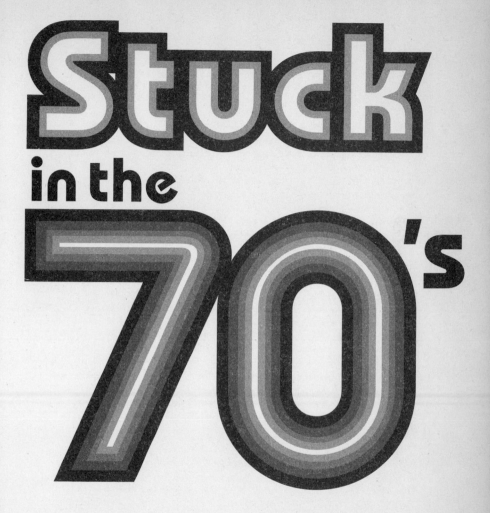

Stuck in the 70's

D. L. Garfinkle

G. P. Putnam's Sons

G. P. PUTNAM'S SONS

A division of Penguin Young Readers Group. Published by The Penguin Group.

Penguin Group (USA) Inc., 375 Hudson Street, New York, NY 10014, U.S.A.

Penguin Group (Canada), 90 Eglinton Avenue East, Suite 700, Toronto, Ontario,
Canada M4P 2Y3 (a division of Pearson Penguin Canada Inc.).

Penguin Books Ltd, 80 Strand, London WC2R 0RL, England.

Penguin Ireland, 25 St. Stephen's Green, Dublin 2, Ireland (a division of Penguin Books Ltd.).

Penguin Group (Australia), 250 Camberwell Road, Camberwell, Victoria 3124, Australia
(a division of Pearson Australia Group Pty Ltd).

Penguin Books India Pvt Ltd, 11 Community Centre, Panchsheel Park,
New Delhi—110 017, India.

Penguin Group (NZ), Cnr Airborne and Rosedale Roads, Albany, Auckland 1310, New Zealand
(a division of Pearson New Zealand Ltd).

Penguin Books (South Africa) (Pty) Ltd, 24 Sturdee Avenue, Rosebank,
Johannesburg 2196, South Africa.

Penguin Books Ltd, Registered Offices: 80 Strand, London WC2R 0RL, England.

Library of Congress Cataloging-in-Publication Data
Garfinkle, D. L. (Debra L.) Stuck in the 70's / D. L. Garfinkle. p. cm.
Summary: A spoiled, rich, seventeen-year-old girl is mysteriously transported from 2006 Los
Angeles back to 1978, where she meets Tyler, a super-smart high school senior who promises
to help her return to 2006 if she will give him some lessons on how to be popular.
[1. Popularity—Fiction. 2. Time travel—Fiction. 3. Feminism—Fiction. 4. High schools—
Fiction. 5. Schools—Fiction. 6. Nineteen seventies—Fiction. 7. Los Angeles (Calif.)—Fiction.]
I. Title. II. Title: Stuck in the seventies.
PZ7.G17975Stu 2007   [Fic]—dc22   2006034460

ISBN 978-0-399-24663-0
10 9 8 7 6 5 4 3 2 1
First Impression

To Judy Green, world's greatest mother,
who has stuck by me always.

Acknowledgments

It's embarrassing how many terrific writer friends I needed to critique this manuscript, including Cieran Blumenthal, Diane Davis, Jody Feldman, Paige Feldman, Collyn Justus, Martha Peaslee Levine, Mary Beth Miller, Elizabeth Paterras, Marlene Perez, Lori Polydoros, Kate Tuthill, and Tony Varrato. I appreciate their helpful advice and blame them entirely for all flaws in this book.

I'm grateful for Judy Green, April Holland, and Lane Klein, who are not only wonderful relatives but do great unpaid PR.

I thank my agent Laura Rennert for making everything seem easy.

And thanks to John Rudolph—kind person, insightful editor, and user of much red ink.

I'm grateful to my husband, Jeff Garfinkle. After the normal government lawyer he married turned into an obsessed fiction writer, he hardly ever complained.

And I thank my children, who on a daily basis confirm my belief in miracles.

There's a beautiful naked girl sitting in my bathtub. It's two A.M. and the splashing woke me. Or did it? Maybe I'm dreaming. I blink my eyes about fifty times. She's still there. Still—blond-haired, thin-armed, and round-breasted—very much there. Even with L.A.'s inferior water quality, I can see her clearly. And clearly she's gorgeous. Just a few melting bubbles play on her shiny skin.

Oh, to be one of those bubbles. One clings to her knee, which pokes above the waterline. The girl's head is thrown back. Her neck is smooth and pale and long. She holds a champagne glass in the air as if she's making a toast. Her eyes are closed, but I don't think she's asleep. Possibly she's meditating. Possibly she's stoned.

I do what any heterosexual seventeen-year-old guy would do: stand frozen at the door with my mouth open and gawk.

Maybe not any heterosexual teenage guy. For instance, if I were a confident, popular guy like Rick The Dick Bowden, I'd probably strip off my L.A. Rams pajamas and join her in the bathtub. Not that The Dick would even own L.A. Rams pajamas. He probably wears a maroon smoking jacket like Hugh Hefner or sleeps in the buff.

Maybe God's answering my prayers in a big way. Or

this could be a practical joke, an excellent one. Or a present. Christmas is coming soon, but I can't think who would give me a gift like this. My best friend, Evie, wouldn't do this. The last present she gave me was a glow-in-the-dark calculator, which was very cool, but geek-cool, not cool in the same way a naked girl in your bathtub is cool.

Given the choice, I'd pick the naked girl.

She opens her eyes. They're Darth Vader black, very soulful and weary.

My heart is going crazy. I think I'm in love.

She looks at me, at the red wallpaper behind me, then finally out the small window at the end of the bathroom. It's as if she's searching for something, yearning and needful.

I try not to ogle her body, but I can't help it. I ask the girl, "How can I help you?"

Her voice is velvet and I almost miss the words. "Who the hell are you?"

She looks around, as if expecting to see people hiding behind the toilet or crouched against the bathroom cupboards. "Jake? Mariel? Where am I? What happened to the Jacuzzi tub? And what is that on the walls?"

I don't know what to say.

"Is that wallpaper, like, fuzzy, or am I completely wasted?"

"Both, probably," I say. "You're wasted and the wallpaper's flocked."

"Flocked?" Then she starts shaking with laughter. Every part of her shakes, most importantly her breasts.

2

I stare at the wall. "It's new wallpaper. My mom picked it out. She wanted to modernize the room." Wow, do I sound like a dork.

"This is how your mom modernizes the room?" she asks. "That wallpaper is, like, total seventies."

"Yes," I say. "That's the point. This room actually used to be pink and black, which my mother says was popular in the fifties." My heartbeat has slowed down, finally. Hearing me pontificate on room renovation could drag the life out of anything.

I feel brave enough to look at her again and force my jaw not to drop. Now I notice her smooth skin the color of Pringles and a scent fresh as—well, fresh as someone in a mildly bubbly bathtub.

"So, what, your mom's like a Martha Stewart?"

"Who's Martha Stewart? My brain isn't exactly in top condition at two in the morning," I say.

"It's two A.M.?"

"Not exactly. It was approximately two seventeen when I got out of bed a few minutes ago." Nerd alert! Nerd alert!

"What the hell went on today?" She blinks like crazy. Is she about to cry? Please, no. I won't be able to stand it. Not that girls cry in front of me all the time, but when it happens it kills me. Cheryl Thompson cried in Honors Algebra class after she got caught looking at my test answers. I hear Mom cry in her bedroom sometimes.

"So who's Martha Stewart?" I say, hoping to get the girl's mind off whatever is giving her the urge to cry.

She swipes her eyes with her hands, and I get to see a close-up view of her breasts—both of them, completely unblocked. They're the greatest, most fantastic, amazing sight I've ever seen. Or probably ever will see.

"Martha Stewart. That zillionaire who makes her own soap and stuff," she says.

I nod, but have no idea who she's talking about.

She sniffs in, big, as if taking back all the potential sobs and saving them for someone more worthwhile. "I need to get out of this damn tub."

"Of course." *No! Please, God, stay!*

"Can you get me a clean towel? Large and fluffy, preferby. Ferably." She's obviously drunk as a skunk. Finally, she pronounces the word properly—"pre-fer-a-bly"—spending approximately three seconds per correctly enunciated syllable.

"I'll bring you a towel."

"I still don't get this seventies look in here. What about 2006?" She shakes her head.

To stave off a possible heart attack, I have to look away again. Yikes! I'm facing the mirror and staring at the naked girl's reflection.

I close my eyes. "In 2006, they might not even use wallpaper. Perhaps thirty years in the future they'll just project holographic beams onto walls."

"Thirty years? Are you drunk too?"

"Twenty-eight years, actually," I say. "Two thousand six minus 1978. Equals twenty-eight years." Help! Geek on the loose!

"It's 1978?"

"Yes." I hold myself back from saying *duh*.

"You're telling me I'm no longer at Jake's house, it's no longer daytime, and it's no longer 2006? I'm in a stranger's house, in the middle of the night, thirty years before 2006?"

"Actually, twenty-eight years."

"This is so not funny anymore. Jake? Mariel? Mom? Where's my cell phone?"

"What's a cell phone?"

"Please, just get me a towel and then get me the hell out of here."

I rush to the linen closet and pray that the girl will still be in my bathtub when I return.

I'm sitting on a furry gold toilet lid, wrapped up in a thin *Jaws* beach towel and slapping my cheeks, hoping to sober up from a horrible hallucination. I put my hand on the wall and feel fuzz, or flock as the guy calls it, and tell myself I'm never drinking again.

What the hell happened tonight? *Think, Shay, think.* My head hurts. I close my eyes.

The last thing I remember, I was in Jake's Jacuzzi tub. His parents', really, and Mariel was yelling at me in Spanish. That was it. Nothing, like, incredibly strange. So how did I end up here? And what's with this boy telling me it's 1978? *Think, Shay.*

There's a knock on the door and a whisper. "It's me. Tyler."

Now what?

I crack open the door.

He's got a big fugly T-shirt neatly folded in his arms. "You can wear this for now. Come into my room and we can rap."

"Rap?"

"You know. Work it out."

I shake my head. "I'm not having sex with you."

"I didn't." He blushes, big-time. "That's not. What I. That's not what I meant."

Sure he didn't. I may not know much, but I know guys. I shove the bathroom door closed, leaving him out in the hall.

But I don't come out of the hallucination, and Jake doesn't rescue me. So I put on the fugly shirt and make my way to Tyler's room. He's sitting on his twin bed with the light on.

"I don't want to rap or whatever," I tell him. "Can I just sleep this off and find my way home when it gets light out?"

"Sure." He pats his bed.

I stay in the doorway. "We're not sharing your bed."

He sighs. "I'll get a blanket and sleep on the floor."

So I lie on Tyler's bed with my face to the wall, hoping this dude won't turn out to be a mass murderer or something, though I doubt murderers let their victims borrow their clothes. I want to sleep, but I can't. *How did I get here?* In this boy's house, in between these scratchy, cheap sheets. I bet the thread count of these sheets is barely in the triple digits. And I'm not used to wearing a T-shirt to bed. It's nowhere near as comfortable as silk.

I close my eyes and try to figure out how this happened. I was late to school yesterday, I know that much. Blame it on my hair. After a major effort of drying, moussing, and combing, it still looked scraggly and wild. A bad hair day is always a sign that the next twenty-four hours will suck.

So, yesterday morning. Nothing too bizarre happened. School was its usual bore. While my teachers droned, I wrote a bunch of lists. Must-haves: black cashmere sweater, more thongs, a purse like in this month's *Vogue*. To-do list:

pedicure, new cell phone ringer, eyebrows, my birthday party invites.

Things got more interesting at lunchtime when I drove to Jake's house. I ate too much pizza there. Two monster slices of sausage and olive, before Jake started kissing me at the kitchen counter.

Is that why I feel so sick? From all the meat and cheese and carbs in me? Not just from the booze?

Jake looted his parents' champagne from the fridge. He said it was, like, three years old. Obviously, his rentals won't miss it.

We got a couple of glasses and took everything upstairs. Jake made a toast to fantastic sex, which I thought was kind of tacky, besides being wishful thinking. But then we got naked and got in the tub and fooled around. I never did it in a Jacuzzi bath before. Can't say I was particularly impressed. Though the Jacuzzi itself was nice. Especially compared to the little tub I awoke in tonight.

Jake and I were still in the Jacuzzi when the doorbell rang, and kept on ringing, like, forever.

Jake went, "What the hell?" He got out, threw on the only decent-size towel in the bathroom, and headed for the front door.

Only a little hand towel remained for me. I'm thin, but not that thin. So I poured myself another glass of champagne and lounged in the tub.

Jake came back upstairs, half-staggering from the champagne/sex combo, but still hot. Jake Robbins probably has the best legs of any guy in the senior class. Long, muscular, hairy but not gorilla-hairy. He stood beside the Jacuzzi, ogling my boobs as I sipped the champagne. "This lady Mariel's downstairs, asking for you. She's all pissed off," he said. "I pretended like I didn't know you, but she recognizes your Jag out front."

I rolled my eyes. I couldn't believe she drove around looking for my car. She's always after me. None of our old housekeepers cared what I did.

I said to Jake, "It's just our housekeeper. No biggie. Tell her I'll be home in an hour or so."

But a minute later Mariel stomped upstairs and threw open the bathroom door. She didn't even pause when she saw me naked. "What you do? The school call look for you," she said.

"Do you mind?" I sank my body into the bubbly water. "My mother isn't paying you to be a damn detective."

She crossed her arms. An attempt to look tough, I guess. Which went nowhere, since Mariel is shrimpy and pudgy and barely speaks English. "I am not pay so much to put up with you, crazy girl."

In her barely literate way, she's right. I feel bad for her, with her broken English and cheap clothes, and badly drawn dragonfly tattoo on her wrist, and total lack of job options, obviously, since she has to work for my mom.

None of the other housekeepers lasted as long as Mariel, and she's only been with us about a year and a half. There were lots of them before her. Anita, Rosa, Guttermouth Gloria, what'sherface who stole, and what'shername who I made cry. My mom should start shelling out more money, like six figures, so she can keep someone around me for a change.

Plus, even with all her stomping around, I think Mariel really likes me for some dumb reason. I could be wrong. She could be faking it for the sake of the job. My own mother doesn't want to hang with me, so why would Mariel?

I looked past her and said, "Get me a towel, Jake."

He stood in the hallway, still half-naked, peeking in on us. All guys love a girlfight.

"Big and fluffy. Please."

He licked his lips, then walked down the hall.

Mariel was still scowling. "Hurry and put on the clothes and come to home. Is no good what you do. Your mother got to be mad."

"You better not tell her," I said. "She'll blame you for not watching me close enough, and she'll look for another housekeeper or whatever, and you'll be out of a job."

"Loca!" Mariel shouted, *loca* being the first of, like, ten Spanish insults she hurled at me as I sat in the bathtub. I knew exactly what they meant, thanks especially to Guttermouth Gloria. I yelled right back at Mariel in Spanish and Spanglish, louder and dirtier. One good thing about Mom pawning me off to housekeepers all my life is that I can speak Spanish.

But soon I got a headache. Either from her yelling or mine, or maybe it was the champagne. I closed my eyes and put my hand over my forehead, grinning through Mariel's attack. Coming from her—all, like, five feet of her, in her high voice—it almost sounded cute.

That's the last thing I remember at Jake's house. Next thing I knew, I was in a different tub, half as small as the Jacuzzi bath. And a boy was hanging over me, and it wasn't Jake, and he was claiming it's 1978.

What the hell was in that champagne?

3

A beautiful girl has been (1) in my bed for over four hours, (2) wearing my favorite T-shirt, (3) *not* wearing any underwear.

This could be a prank. Am I on *Candid Camera*? I doubt it. Allen Funt might put a girl in someone's house, but not a naked one.

I wish I had this on camera. Recorded evidence that a beautiful girl spent the night in my room would probably do wonders for my social standing, or lack thereof. No one would believe me otherwise. Except Evie, of course, but she doesn't count.

The girl stays half under my sheet, propped on one elbow, obviously still braless, and stares at me. She's gorgeous even in the morning, with her blond hair frizzy and untamed around her face, which is pale as typing paper.

"What if your mom or dad comes in?" she asks while I load my backpack for school.

"They respect my space."

"What, you mean your parents ignore you too?" She laughs. "I need a toothbrush and a hairbrush. New ones, please. And coffee. I could so use a grande nonfat latte from Starbucks right now."

"What's Starbucks?"

"Good one," she says. "Look, if we're pretending it's 1978, we should take your Pinto or Ford station wagon or whatever, and drive up to Seattle and see if you can invest in Starbucks coffee." She bites her lip. "I'm still in California, aren't I?"

"Yes, of course. The Valley. But I don't own a car."

"You got to be kidding."

I don't care how sexy she is, my hospitality is wearing thin. I glance at my digital alarm clock. Eleven minutes until I need to leave.

She sits all the way up in my bed.

Okay, I do care how sexy she is. Her breasts are fantastic. Like ripe grapefruit. Their shape, anyway. I doubt they have a bumpy peel or sour taste. I can't think about the taste or I'll lose all semblance of control. But, man, her breasts.

Too bad she can't stay. I'll tell my parents and they'll straighten this out. She's either a runaway or crazy or both. But she doesn't look crazy. Certainly not like Linda Blair in *The Exorcist*, or any of the Manson girls.

"Can you peel your eyes off me for a second and get me a new toothbrush, a hairbrush, and coffee?"

I force my gaze away, to my Einstein poster on the wall behind her. What would Einstein do? For one thing, if he wanted to impress a gorgeous girl in his bedroom, he wouldn't hang a picture of a physicist on his wall.

Think, Tyler, think. Einstein said kindness, beauty, and

truth are the most important things in life. So I should be kind to this beautiful girl, but tell my parents the truth.

I check the digital clock again. Nine more minutes. "I'll look for a toothbrush and comb."

"Brush," she says. "A new brush if you can find one. And I have to drink some coffee."

"How you doing, kids?" Mom calls from downstairs.

"Fine!" I squeal.

"Kids?" the girl asks.

"Has anyone seen my pocket dictionary?" Heather yells from her room.

"Not me!" I respond in my new, unintentional Mickey Mouse voice. "Your dictionary's definitely not in my room."

"You have a sister?"

"Shh. Yes. Let me find those things for you."

I leave the room and run downstairs. I see Mom in the kitchen, but I can't bring myself to tell her about the girl I'm hiding, not just yet. With four minutes to spare until official school departure time, I manage a new tooth-brush, a used comb rinsed out in the bathroom sink, a can of soda, and a sesame seed bagel.

I race upstairs. She's still in my bed, the sheet now lowered to the level of her hips. I try to suppress my grin while handing her the bagel. "I couldn't find coffee." I give her the soda. "I think this has caffeine."

"What's that?"

"Tab."

She peers at the hot pink label. "That's a diet soda? Huh."

She takes a bite from the bagel, scattering crumbs all over my blanket. "I need some underwear at least, and a bra would be nice."

No bra! I plead silently. "You could try my sister's room for, uh, a brassiere. It's right next to my room. Heather goes to school the same time I do." I avoid looking at the girl's chest, which I know will never squeeze into my sister's bras. Or my mom's for that matter. Ugh. No boy should have to picture the girl he lusts after in his mother's brassiere. "Just stay in my room. You can come out after ten forty-five. My mom always has a hairdresser appointment at eleven on Wednesdays, and then lunch with her girlfriends. The house should be free for two and a half hours at least."

What am I saying? I'm going to leave her alone in my house? What if she steals everything we own? Our nineteen-inch color TV? My Commodore computer, which took me over ninety hours to construct?

"Don't leave me alone," she says.

I shake my head. "I have to get to school. I can try to help you afterward."

"Please." She stretches her legs beneath my blanket. Holy cow, they're long.

"Maybe I can leave school early," I tell her.

"It's easy. I cut classes all the time. *Caveat emptor.*"

"Buyer beware?"

She shakes her head. "Seize the day."

"That's *carpe diem*."

"Whatever. Just act like you have somewhere important to go. Walk fast through the halls and hold your head high."

"I'm applying to colleges soon. I can't afford to get in trouble."

She bites her lip again. It's an alluring look for her. But then again, what isn't?

"Okay, I'll try to get home early for you," I say. I mean it.

4

After Tyler leaves, I snoop around his bedroom like I'm on *Room Raiders*. A girl can learn a lot from the contents of a guy's room. For instance, Jake has *Penthouse* magazines and baggies of weed in his closet, and condoms hidden under his bed.

Tyler has a poster of Albert Einstein's hairy head, and another of a very young Robin Williams with a perky brunette girl, captioned *Nanu, Nanu*. The bed I slept in is covered by a *Star Wars* blanket. Under the bed is a teddy bear. Sweet. A neat desk is occupied by a humongous, antique computer. Above it are shelves crammed with books—literary crap, textbooks, and a bunch of books about Einstein: *The Man Behind the Math, Albert Speaks, The Greatest Mind Ever.*

Just when I've pegged him for a total dweeb, I see a *Charlie's Angels* calendar. It's from the old TV show, not the movie remake, and it's definitely from 1978. There's nothing here—no iPod, DVD player, cordless phone—to prove I'm not in 1978.

I'm getting freaked out.

I open and close dresser drawers. He wears briefs. I knew he wasn't the boxers type.

I move to his closet and leaf through a few boxes containing a baseball card collection. All the cards are really old, nothing later than 1978.

In the back corner of the closet I find a plastic pitcher. It's heavy. Coins clank inside it. I've hit upon Tyler's stash.

I can't help myself. I pull the lid off the top of the pitcher and shake out the money. I reach in with my fingers to make sure I've gotten all the bills. He has mostly coins, but also a lot of ones folded neatly in half, two fives, and a twenty. They're all old bills with dull faces. Maybe he inherited them from someone. I lay the paper money on the rug and count it. Forty-six dollars.

My purse still must be at Jake's house. Gawd, I hope no one stole it.

I put the coins back in the bank and hold the bills. I wouldn't take Tyler's money unless I absolutely needed it. He got me a towel last night, let me sleep in his bed without attempting a pass, found me that Tab drink and a toothbrush.

But it's not like I have my own money here. Besides, how do I know Tyler didn't steal my purse? Maybe he kidnapped me yesterday and took me to his house. Maybe the nice-guy image is all just an act.

I hide the bills under Tyler's mattress and return the pitcher to the back of the closet. To keep my mind off my guilt, I look through the closet again. I pick up an old junior high yearbook from 1976. Not my school, but a feeder to my high school. If it really were 1978 now, Tyler's picture could be in the book.

I leaf through the yearbook, telling myself it's only because there's nothing else to do. The boys have hangdog hair. The girls wear theirs either long and droopy, or cropped to stick out like a wedge of hard cheese. Both sexes wear wide, clownish collars.

There are handwritten notes, though not anywhere near as many as in my middle school yearbook. *Tyler, Thanks for all your help in geometry. From, Cindy; To Tyler Gray, one of the smartest guys I know. Louise; Tyler, Sorry about the spitwads. Thanks for the science tutoring. I hope I'm in more classes with you next year. Larry.*

His picture's with the ninth-grade class, captioned *Tyler Gray.*

I'm getting even more freaked out.

Computer trick, I tell myself. Clever. Or maybe that's his dad. The Tyler I met might really be Tyler Gray, Jr. Or Tyler Gray the Second. Whatever. It's not his picture.

Or I could be on *Punk'd.* A new, non-celebrity version. I look around for cameras. Maybe they're hidden in that oversized computer. "Is this a trick?" I whisper into the computer. "It's getting old."

No response.

A camera lens on the ceiling?

No. Just that ugly popcorn stuff which is probably crawling with asbestos.

"Jake? Mariel?" I call out softly.

Nothing.

I take three deep breaths, clutch the yearbook to my chest, and return to Tyler's bed.

I flip through the book for more Tyler sightings. He was in Honor Society and backgammon club. There's a long note next to a picture of a grinning, flat-chested, skinny girl holding up a trophy. The sloppy handwriting is in orange ink. *Here's to lots more backgammon championships,* it says. It lists all these geeky memories like *I'll never forget that 7-hour backgammon marathon we played, or that time we snuck into the computer lab.* Blah blah blah. *Love, your best friend, Evie.*

I can't believe I'm reading all this. I'd never hang with the guy, normally. But in this situation, whatever it is, I guess it's better to end up at a semi-dork's house than, like, a felon's. He even trusts me in his bedroom. Dumb of him.

5

"*You'd be a fool* to cut classes for a girl," Evie says as we walk to English class.

"Normally, I'd agree. But this girl is gorgeous. Need I remind you I saw her naked?"

"You needn't. Please."

I elbow her. "Oh, sheesh, look who's coming."

Plowing down the hallway is Rick The Dick, next to a guy who looks like a giant Weeble.

Evie shrugs. "I'm not worried."

"Watch out!"

The Weeble's globular leg sticks out in front of us. I stop walking just in time, but Evie topples onto her face.

I pull her up and hand her glasses to her. Then I glare at the laughing Weeble. "Be careful."

"Sorry," The Dick says as he and his friend continue down the hallway.

"Sure he's sorry. It wasn't even his leg sticking out. I bet The Dick's friend weighs two and a half times as much as you," I tell Evie.

She examines her glasses. "I'd rather be smart than big. I bet my IQ is fifty points higher than his."

"You're a genius. I know, I know."

She punches my arm playfully. Not that she could

have packed any power even if she'd wanted to. To Evie's annoyance, she's never broken five feet or a hundred pounds. I'm not sure what's worse for her social life: her small size, her intelligence, or the fact that she doesn't seem to mind being in the out crowd.

"High IQs don't help us in the school hallways," I tell her. "We should try to fit in better so the jerks won't pick on us so much."

"It's mostly me they pick on." She puts on her glasses and resumes walking. "I have no inclination to fit in."

"You should. This is our last year here, Evie, our last chance for popularity. When I look back on my high school years, I want to remember at least a few parties and girls, not just physics class and backgammon." I nudge her. "Look at that foxy girl walking toward us. I think she's actually staring at me."

The girl points to Evie's ankles. "Waiting for a flood?"

"Okay, maybe she wasn't staring at me," I say.

"We'll never be cool," Evie says. "Not in a googolplex years."

"We've got to try. Hey, maybe I should grow a moustache like Burt Reynolds and my dad. They're both pretty cool."

"You should concentrate on growing your GPA. You look cute as you are, Tyler."

"Cute? Hardly. Even if I am, mere cuteness won't make me popular. Evie, I don't want that girl in my house finding out about my poor social ranking."

"She probably already knows. I bet someone just planted her in your bathtub as a sick joke to make an Honors Society student ditch school."

I shake my head and picture the girl in my room, waiting for me, still braless.

"Eighty to one odds she won't be there when you get home," Evie says. "Probably as we speak, she and her friends are laughing about the stunt they pulled. Do you think it's one of the cheerleaders? Last week, this cheerleader—"

"I hope she isn't going through my stuff."

"Tyler?"

"What if she finds my teddy bear?"

"Earth to Tyler."

"Did you say something?"

Evie shakes her head. "She's got you, hook, line, and sinker."

I smile. "I want to be scaled, boned, and eaten."

Huh? Why is Robin Williams staring at me?

It's a poster, and oh my gawd, I'm still in this weird house. I must have fallen asleep.

The giant digital alarm clock says it's already 11:06. Tyler's mom should be gone by now. Time to get out of here.

I pull down Tyler's robe from the hook on the closet door and wrap it around me. It has a nice musky smell. I head to the bathroom.

Damn. Same bathroom as early this morning. Why can't this be just a bad dream? Splashing water on my face does nothing but get me wet. At least I haven't lost my looks here, according to the mirror.

I flee the bathroom and tiptoe down the stairs, passing more of that red flocked wallpaper. The carpet downstairs is gold and shaggy. In the tiny living room is one of those La-Z-Boys or Barcaloungers or whatever, with a newspaper on it.

It's the *Los Angeles Times*, dated September 27, 1978. On the front page: "The Bee Gees Storm the States" and "President Carter Urges Energy Conservation." Ads show the grand opening of a new Typewriter City and $60,000 houses for sale in L.A. Someone's pulled out all the stops for this joke. The newspaper pages aren't even yellowed.

"Good one! But I'm so onto you!" My voice trembles.

There's no response. I look for camera lenses again, but come up empty.

I walk into the little kitchen, ugly and dated with its olive green counters and floor of gold-tinged linoleum or vinyl or something equally awful. The room is spotless. On the counter is an old-fashioned phone with a curly cord and a dial.

I call my house.

"Hello?" Some man answers.

Mom has a new guy? "Is Camelia Saunders there?"

"You got the wrong number."

"How about Shay Saunders?"

"I never heard of no Saunders," he says and hangs up. I put

the phone on the cradle. Then I pick it up again, hear a dial tone, bite my lip, and redial my number.

"Hello?" Same guy.

"Is my mom there? It's Shay, her daughter. Shay Saunders."

"I told you. There's no Saunders here."

"Is this 448-0475?"

"Yeah, but there's no Saunders here. Stop calling."

So I hang up, then dial my number one more time.

"Yeah?"

"Sorry to bother—"

"Knock it off, you crazy bitch." He hangs up on me.

What the hell is going on? Has my whole family been kidnapped? If you can call me and my mom a whole family. Did my mom decide to get rid of me?

Wandering into the living room doesn't give me any answers. The TV has a dial on it too. I push the *On* button and change channels. Bizarre versions of *That '70s Show* play on every station. There are only five of them. *The Price Is Right* is hosted by a young Bob Barker in a bright orange suit and fat tie, and an ancient *General Hospital* features skinny ladies in miniskirts and moustached men with permed hair.

It has to be a trick. "Who's doing this? One of my friends?" I try to laugh like a good sport, but my high-pitched "ha" just sounds scared. "Come on out already."

No one comes out.

It's a big setup. Time travel is something you see in romance movies with fancy old costumes, or read about as a kid so the author can feed you history lessons. Time travel is not real.

"Great joke," I announce. "Is this, like, senior-class prank or an early surprise birthday party?"

Nothing but happy screams from the TV set. On *The Price Is Right*, a girl with a Farrah Fawcett haircut and bright green eyeshadow just won a brand-new King Cobra Mustang, valued at $6,803.

I need chocolate. Fast.

I go back to the kitchen. The cupboards are full of weird boxes and cans of food with no nutrition labels on them. A large bag of raisins is stamped "Best used before 12/28/78." Behind it is a package of Oreos, stamped "Purchase before 1/8/79." The Oreos taste fine. Except I like Double Stuf better.

At first I untwist each cookie, eat the filling, and gobble up the sandwich part. After the first few cookies, I start cramming them in my mouth, one after another, no longer tasting them, but feeling their fullness inside me. I use my fingernails to pick up the crumbs which fall on my legs. I eat the crumbs too. "Mariel? Jake? Mom!" I call out with my mouth stuffed, but no one answers.

6

I can't believe it. I'm ditching the last two periods of school. Me, who hasn't even been tardy since last winter when Mike Kagey threw my binder in the mud. I'm walking quickly with my head up like I have confidence, just like the girl told me to do.

"Tyler!" Evie shouts. She's coming down the hall from the other direction. She's quick, especially considering her backpack probably weighs twenty pounds. "I thought you're in Building G fifth period. Why are you walking that way?" she asks.

I put my finger to my lips. With my luck, a teacher will hear Evie and question me about my destination. Though I imagine I'd be the last person a teacher would suspect of ditching school. Actually, Evie would be the last person. I'd be second to last.

"Tyler Gray. Wait up, dude."

Oh, no. Is that who I think it is? I stop and turn my head.

Yes, it is. Principal Shipper's a few yards behind me. I instantly lose my display of fake confidence.

"Pat!" Evie runs over to us, waving her arms.

Even I know it's the antithesis of cool to run *to* a principal. Principal Shipper wears bright bead necklaces, says "Keep on truckin" at the end of his morning P.A. announcements, and asks everyone to call him Pat. But he's still a principal and therefore will never be cool.

"Hey, Pat." Evie approaches us. "Thanks for restoring the budget for the Honor Society banquet."

In front of me, Debbie M. says, "Dip and Drip," to Debbie P., and they both giggle.

"So, Tyler, why are you heading this way?" Evie says.

I wonder if Principal Shipper suspects anything fishy. I wonder how red my face is right now.

"Don't you have German class in Building G?" Evie asks.

I wonder how I'm going to answer this.

"Tyler? You still distracted by that girl?"

Oh, no. Now she's bringing up the girl in my bedroom. "I . . . I'm walking this way to . . . to try to talk to someone."

"A chick?" the principal asks.

I try not to roll my eyes. "Actually, I probably don't have time, anyway."

"Don't be shy around the *chicas*," he says. "They love the honor students."

Now I do roll my eyes at that one.

"You should just go toward Building G," Evie tells me. "Neither one of us has gotten so much as a tardy all year," she tells the principal.

"Okay, I'm off to German class." I turn around and rush off, keeping my perfect school record intact but breaking my promise to the girl.

* * *

After downing half the package of Oreos, I lean back on the couch and try to figure things out. Everything in this house is decades old. Maybe Tyler's family just wants to live like they're in the 70's, even though they're not.

Wait! I'll go outside. Of course. I'll see Hummers, in-line skates, tile roofs, and people with piercings carrying iPods. I'll borrow a cell phone so I can call for help. I'd better get some clothes on first.

I find an ugly skirt in the master bedroom closet, then run toward the front door and pull it open.

No! I stand at the doorway and stare across the street. A seventies Oldsmobile sits in front of an old olive green, shingle-roofed house.

I walk outside. Parked in driveways and lining the curbs are cars from the 60's and 70's—woody station wagons, purple Pintos, an orange, boxy Volkswagen van full of old bumper stickers like *Carter-Mondale* and *Pass ERA Now*. A lady across the street is pruning roses. She wears a "1976—America's Bicentennial" T-shirt.

No, no, no.

I creep back inside and slam the door closed, as if that will keep the 70's away.

But they've already invaded Tyler's house. My knees feel wobbly and my breaths are shallow. Why was I put here? I wasn't even alive in 1978. How do I get home? Maybe the same way I got here?

I go upstairs and lie in the empty tub, still dressed in Tyler's fugly T-shirt and his mother's gawdawful skirt. No underwear, though. Even if it's clean, wearing someone else's panties is gross. And old lady underwear would be hard to take, after wearing only thongs the last few years.

I close my eyes and wish myself into 2006.

Nothing happens.

I whisper, "Please, please, please."

Nada.

I even pray for the first time in my life. "God, please, I won't sleep around so much, and not ever again with someone else's boyfriend, even if I don't like the girl. Except if she's a real bitch, I might. I don't think You'd mind that, God. And I won't cut school—not as often, anyway—or draw any more pictures on the whiteboard of my biology teacher kissing the class lizard."

I look up to heaven, which hopefully exists above the beige asbestos ceiling, and wait.

Zippo.

"Please, God, I'm scared now." I press my palms together, the tips of my fingers touching my chin, my elbows sore against the hard edge of the bathtub. I'm a real suppicant, or however you say that word.

I hear something.

My heart pounds under the borrowed T-shirt. "God, is that You?" I whisper. "Or, like, one of Your angels? Or angels-in-training, like Clarence in *It's a Wonderful Life*, which always makes me cry, I swear to it, God."

It's a beautiful voice, singing "You-hoo-hoo light up myyyyy life."

So there is a God! And I was right. She's female.

"Thank you, thank you, God. You light up my life too. Can I please go home now, God?"

Someone is singing along. It's a woman, sounding scratchy and off-key.

Then a male voice comes on, announcing we've just heard the hot, hot, hot Bee Gees, sparkling Neil Diamond, and sweet Debby Boone, singing her number one song, "You Light Up My Life."

Gawd. Tyler's mom must be home, listening to the radio.

"Thanks for nothing, God. Except for ending that stupid song." I climb out of the bathtub.

Downstairs, another tune plays and Tyler's mother wails, "You'd think I could learrrn how to tell you good-bye, 'cause you don't bring me flowers aaaaanymooooore."

I sink back into the tub and stare at the asbestos ceiling. "God," I whisper. "I think I'm really stuck in the damn seventies. Please get me the hell out of here. And hurry."

7

I rush home from the bus stop to see if the girl is still in my house. Or if the house is still standing.

Mom meets me at the front door before I can dart upstairs. She kisses me on the cheek. She wouldn't kiss me if she'd just discovered a half-naked girl in my room, or the TV and stereo system missing. Would she?

I can't help glancing at the stairs. All quiet. Evie's likely right. The girl's probably long gone by now. I never even got her name.

"Aren't you going to say something?" Mom's standing in front of me with her arms crossed.

Uh-oh. I eye the staircase again, wondering what the girl has done.

"Look at me," Mom says.

I can do it, but not in the eyes. So I stare at Mom's nose. I can't help noticing a strong chemical odor. Did the girl start a fire in here?

"Something's different," Mom says.

I gulp, audibly, then try to cover with a throat clear. "Why do you say something's different?" I'm trying too hard to sound innocent, like those witnesses on *Perry Mason* right before they confess their heinous crimes in open court.

"Didn't you notice? I got a haircut. And a perm."

Phew.

She touches the side of her head, which I only now realize has expanded two to three inches due to hair frizz. "Perms are all the rage now. I hope your father likes it."

I let out a big breath, as if I haven't exhaled since I got off the bus. I might not have, actually. Dad won't like Mom's perm. Then again, Dad doesn't like much of anything. Then again again, Dad probably won't even notice Mom's hair. I hope for her sake the chemical stench dissipates soon.

"So what do you think of my new 'do?"

"It looks good, Mom. I'm going to put my books upstairs now."

"Wait," Mom says just as I reach the stairs.

Now what?

"Did you get up in the middle of the night?"

Erase that prior *phew*. "Huh?"

"A midnight snack or something?"

I look her in the nose again and slowly nod.

"Because I just bought a package of Oreos yesterday, and they're already half gone. You ate those, I take it?"

I keep nodding. "Sorry. I won't do it again."

I make a break for it and race up the stairs.

Yes! She's still here. Still beautiful. And in my room. On my very bed. In clothes which cling to her. And she's still braless. Oh, yes! I hold my hand against the door frame to steady myself.

"You didn't come home early like you promised."

"I didn't . . ." Now I'm looking *her* in the nose. Wow,

even her nose is sexy. It's little and smooth, with a cute upswing at the tip of it. "I didn't promise, actually. Not exactly."

"I need help getting home."

"Did you try sitting in the bathtub again?"

"Yeah. It didn't work."

"Um . . . " I clear my throat. "What's your name?"

"Shay. Dumb name, huh?"

"Not at all. Just somewhat rare." I say it to myself. *Shay, Shay, Shay.* My heart is about to burst out of my chest. If she married me, she'd be Shay Gray. Not good. "Tyler's a rare name too," I say.

"Not in the twenty-first century. At my school alone, there are two Tylers playing varsity football this year, and another Tyler is the team mascot."

Twenty-first century? Son of a gun. She really believes she's from the future.

I walk over to her, unsteady in my own room, and sit beside her on my bed. "Shay, my mom said you ate a bunch of Oreos today."

She bites her lip. "You told your mother?"

"No. My mom just said half the package was gone."

"Oh," she murmurs. "It wasn't even Double Stuf."

"Huh?"

"Double Stuf Oreos."

"The Oreo of the future?" This whole fantasy is ridiculous. "I'm going to have to tell my parents soon. I mean, if you keep staying here."

"They won't believe it. No one will believe it." Her dark eyes seem frightened under lashes like heavy black veils. "You probably don't even believe it."

I look away. I don't believe it.

"What if I prove I'm from the future?"

"Go ahead."

"Okay, I was reading the newspaper today."

I can't help arching my eyebrows. She doesn't seem the newspaper-reading type.

"Only to help me figure things out. It's not like I'm a nerd. So I read that Jimmy Carter is president now. I know he barely lasts one period, or term, or whatever." She scrunches her sexy nose. "Because of, I think, the gas crisis and the hostages in Iran. Or Iraq. No, Iran."

"Huh?"

"I took Modern American History last year. I even got a B minus in the class. So when the gas crisis hits, and the hostage thingie, you'll know I'm from the future."

"If you're from the future, why don't you warn the potential hostages?"

"Right." She shakes her head. "I'm sure they'll believe me as much as you do. Like I can even remember their names. Anyway, I don't think any of them die from it. I'm not sure. It's not like I got an A in the class."

"So when does all this actually happen?"

She sighs. "I don't know. Oh, and I have something else. I read in the paper about this new Italian pope."

"And?"

"I think he's the guy that dies."

"Everyone dies. Even popes."

"Don't be a smart-ass. This guy only lasts, like, a month. They elected this Polish guy. Or appointed him, or whatever they do with that white smoke. And *he* just died. I mean, he died, like, in 2004 or 2005, which is my past, your future."

"What?"

"Never mind. Just believe me. Please." She puts her hand on my thigh.

Suddenly it's summertime in the sweltering swamp known as Tylertown. How could a human hand increase the temperature of my leg by twenty degrees? A question for my physics teacher. Though I doubt he has the answer. I doubt any guy has the answer.

"You can keep staying with me," I say to the bedspread.

She removes her hand. I start breathing again.

"I can't hide in your room forever," she says. "You'll have to tell your parents."

"They'll kill me."

"So what's your plan to keep me here?"

I don't have a plan. Or an inkling of a plan. What would Einstein do? Better yet, what would a ladies' man do? What would John Travolta do? Whatever it took to keep a beautiful girl next to him on his bed.

I close my eyes so I can think with my brain. "I could tell my folks you have nowhere else to go."

"They'll buy that?"

"My mom's kind of a pushover. And my dad's hardly ever here, anyway."

I don't mean to sound so sad. She clutches my arm. A pity grip. Still, I'll take it.

"We'll tell them my parents are horrible, that they, like, beat me or something," she says.

I open my eyes. "Do they?"

"Don't be ridiculous. I've never even met my dad." She frowns. "And I doubt my mom will even realize I'm missing yet. If she does, I'm not sure she'll care."

Wow. How could a mom not care? "Well, my mom cares. For one thing, she'll want to make sure you're not a runaway. So we'll have to pretend to call your parents and get permission."

"Cool."

I shake my head. "She'll want to talk to them herself."

"Not cool."

What would Travolta do? "Maybe someone could disguise his voice and pretend to be one of your parents."

Whoa, Tyler. This is getting out of control. Not only will you be lying to Mom, but you'll be bringing in a third party to lie. Is one girl worth messing up your life?

"I love it!" She squeezes my arm again. "You're so smart."

This girl is worth it. "I'll ask my best friend Evie to pretend to be your mother."

"So you're going to let me stay here with your rentals and everything?"

"My rentals?"

"Rental units. It's modern slang for *your parents*. Modern for 2006."

What am I getting myself into? Lying to Mom and Dad so this crazy girl can tell time-travel stories and put her hands all over me? "You can stay as long as you want."

8

"**I never thought I'd** be shopping at a thrift store. Gross," I say.

Tyler grimaces. "A simple 'Thank you for driving me' will do."

We're in a wood-paneled station wagon, which reeks from the strawberry-scented air freshener hanging from the rearview mirror. I'm wearing a sweater from Tyler's sister's room, with Ms. Gray's ugly skirt and socks and sensibly awful flat shoes. And, probably to Tyler's utter joy, no bra. According to the DJ, Barry Manilow, Donna Summer, and The Commodores play on the radio and they're all totally bitchin'. While he drives, Tyler shrugs his shoulders in rhythm to the music. He'd stop bopping around if he knew the girl next to him stole his money. Under my lapbelt there's forty-six dollars in my pocket. I had to take it, right?

I bite my lip and stare out the car window. It's as smoggy now as in 2006. We pass familiar streets—Roscoe, Canoga, Sherman Way. Tyler's house seems close to mine. Not counting the twenty-eight-year time difference.

He parks and we get out of the car.

The customers in the thrift store are dressed worse than I even imagined. "Are they holding auditions here for a fashion makeover show?" I whisper.

"Shh."

"At least I won't see anyone I know. Except maybe, like, my mom or my teachers when they were teens. That would be bizarre." I head to a rack of clothes and touch one of the blouses. "Eww." I wipe my fingers on my skirt, really Tyler's mom's skirt.

"What's wrong?" Tyler asks.

"I just touched polyester for the first time in my life. Whoever put me back in time should have packed me a suitcase."

On the bright side, or at least not totally horrible side, 1978 thrift store prices buy me a lot for $46—shirts, pants, awful shoes, and even a few days' worth of 25-cent-per-piece lingerie, if you could call thrift shop stuff *lingerie*.

Every time I go near the bras and panties, Tyler's face flushes and he has to look away. "Check this out, Tyler." I hold up a bra just to watch his face get redder. "This will have to be washed at least three times before I ever wear it."

He looks away again.

"Will you show me how to use a washing machine? That was always our housekeeper's job."

"You don't know how to do laundry? Even I know how, and I'm a guy."

"Why should I when we're paying Mariel to do that? She tried to show me how to do laundry once. She said it was for my own good. It's not like I want to live with Mom and her forever, so I get Mariel's stab at teaching me Independent Living 101."

"If you have a housekeeper at home, what are you doing at my house?" he asks.

"Like I planned this whole time-travel thing. I hope Mariel didn't freak when I disappeared. Even if Mom hasn't noticed I'm gone, Mariel would." My eyes moisten. I sniff in big so I won't blubber. "I bet Mariel even misses me a little."

He puts his hand on my shoulder. "You all right?"

"Yeah. Sure." I take a step back and dab at my eyes. I'm still holding the bra, which now dangles down my face.

Tyler looks away.

I blink away the puddling tears, lay the bra in the crook of my arm, and hold up two sweaters. "Tyler, which one do you think is less awful, this striped monstrosity or this army blanket thing?"

"Let me ask you something. If you got zapped naked into my bathtub from the future, how are you paying for this stuff?"

Crap. I was hoping he wouldn't think of that. At least I have something prepared. "Whoever sent me into your bathtub put forty dollars in it too."

He smirks. "I don't remember seeing soggy money in the tub with you. And they would have had to give you old bills, right? Because you couldn't use money from the future here. If they even use money in your world."

"Mostly we use credit cards. Yes, luckily, they sent me with old bills."

"Right. Whoever *they* is. In any event, we need to get home for dinner. I promised my mom."

His mom cares about eating dinner together? Strange.

I use the money I stole from Tyler, but I have to look away from him. I stare at my bag of clothes. I don't know if any of this stuff is in style in 1978. It all looks hideous to me. Though the thrift store crap beats what I'm wearing now. "If I'm meeting your family tonight, I need to change out of their clothes," I tell him, and point to the dusty green curtain hanging in the back of the store. "Don't peek."

Tyler's face is bright red. "I . . . "

I wink at him.

He smiles, slightly and guiltily, in return.

"Mom!" I yell from the front door. "I met a friend at the library. Can my friend come over for dinner?"

"Sure, Tyler, invite him over," Mom says from the kitchen.

"It's a *her*, actually." We walk together toward the kitchen. Shay manages to look sexy even in her thrift store blouse and pants.

Mom is at the stove, mashing potatoes. "Evie?" she asks.

"No. Shay," I say.

Mom spins around. Her eyebrows rise a quarter inch above their customary height. Even my own mother can't believe a beautiful girl would want to hang out with me. "Welcome," she says. "How do you two know each other?"

42

"From school." The fib slips out of Shay's mouth like air. "We have a few classes together."

My mother's brows lift another quarter inch.

My cheeks feel so hot that if I were to lie on my side, someone could probably fry an egg on one of them. "I think we just have one class together," I mumble. "Homeroom." I shoot Shay a warning look and notice that the plastic bag of clothes she's carrying has Mom's shoes sticking out on top. I stare purposefully at it. She nods and excuses herself to use the bathroom.

Once she's gone, I take a big breath and start on the whopper. "I feel sorry for her. Her parents are awful. You should see Shay's face when she mentions them. Tears stream down her face, actually."

"What's so awful about them?" Mom asks. "They're obviously poor. That girl needs new clothes."

"I know." I take a deep breath. "Are you aware she's living all by herself?"

"What?"

"It's true. Her parents decided to move to . . . to . . . " Where did they supposedly move to? Shay and I discussed Reno and Vegas. I'm ninety-five percent sure we finally chose Reno, given that it's a lot farther from L.A. Maybe we should have picked Atlantic City.

"Tyler?" Mom's eyebrows head north again.

"Oh, yeah, Reno." I'm a terrible liar. "They left Shay with her aunt in this tiny apartment in . . . Reseda." Shay told me to use lots of details. She didn't say what to do if my face burned up under Mom's hot glare.

"How did you even meet this girl?"

"In homeroom." Details, details. "She sits on my left. My direct left. Anyway, her aunt met this French guy and moved to Paris."

"Paris?" Mom's eyebrows are practically touching her scalp.

The French lover was Shay's idea. "So she's living by herself in this crummy apartment in Reseda."

"How do you know it's crummy? You haven't been there, have you?"

I wish I'd been there. Wait a minute. There *is* no crummy apartment in Reseda, so how could I wish to go there? Well, maybe there is, but Shay doesn't live in it. Actually, I don't know where she lives. "No, Mom, I haven't been to Shay's apartment. She says she's so ashamed of it, she never invites people over."

"Why does she go to your school if she lives in Reseda?"

Shay and I didn't think of that one. "Um, maybe she used to live here. Mom, if you were a man you'd be a great lawyer."

She keeps grilling me. "What are her parents doing in Reno?"

"They're gambling, Mom. If her parents have anything left to gamble. They're both addicts."

"Poor Shay," Mom says.

Bingo. "I know. They even . . . No, this is so awful."

"Even what?"

"Shay feels bad enough."

"Tell me, Tyler."

I go for the kill. "Shay's parents sold her clothes at the swap meet and took the profits to Vegas. I mean, Reno." I'm a big, stinking liar.

"That poor girl! We must have her over for dinner." Mom now has the same expression she wore last month when she found the dead baby bird on our porch. "I noticed how thin she is. She needs some fattening up, the poor dear. And a mother's special touch."

Yes! And how about a son's special touch too?

Tyler's mother is making clucking noises. "You need protein, dear."

Tyler must have told his mom that I have, like, the sorriest rentals who ever existed. Maybe he said my parents starved me. She's threatening me with a giant fork, spearing a thousand-calorie hunk of meat over my plate. I haven't seen so much beef since the Super Bowl.

"You don't like my mother's cooking, Shake?" Tyler's sister asks me.

"It's *Shay,* not Shake," I say.

She shrugs. "Oh, sorry."

I bet. Looks like the Gray nice-gene skipped over Heather.

"Shay," Mr. Gray says as his wife stands behind him spooning buttered noodles onto his plate. "Strange name." This from a man with beef fat clinging to his caterpillar moustache?

Ms. Gray exchanges the noodle dish for the asparagus platter. "Shay is a lovely name."

"Thank you, Ms. Gray."

"Shay, honey, please call me *Mrs.* Gray." She finally sits down and takes a bite of salad. "I'm just not suited to be a Ms." She rises. "More meat, anyone?"

"Hey, Heather, do you have any clothes Shay could borrow?" Tyler asks.

Heather looks at the giant fork as if she's deciding whether to spear me with it.

"That's okay," I say. I went through her closet today. Her clothes are a tiny step up from the thrift store crap.

Mrs. Gray glares at Heather before emitting another cluck. "I'll take you shopping tonight, Shay. I bet you could use a few necessities. Undergarments and such."

Undergarments. That's the cutest word. I don't think I've heard it spoken out loud before today. I can't help smiling.

Mrs. Gray smiles back. So does Tyler, though his borders on a leer. Heather scowls.

Mr. Gray picks up the *L.A. Times* business section from under his chair and mutters about gas reaching 68 cents a gallon. "Another biscuit, Marlene."

Mrs. Gray rushes over with a gingham cloth–covered basket and tongs, and sets a biscuit on his plate.

"You've barely sat down for three seconds," I tell her. "We can get our own food. You don't have to serve us."

"My dad works hard during the day," Tyler says.

"I bet your mom does too. She deserves—"

"Don't start anything between my parents." He glares at me.

At least one of his parents seems totally unfazed. Mr. Gray's buried under the newspaper. "Betamax or Sony?" he mutters.

"Sony," I say.

He exchanges the business section of the paper for another one beneath his chair. "That job didn't last long."

"What job, dear?" Mrs. Gray asks.

"Pope. The new pope just died. The Italian guy. Now they have to have the meetings and the white smoke all over again."

Across the table from me, Tyler freezes with a forkful of pasta suspended in the air and his mouth open like a dentist just told him to say *ah*.

I nod at him. "Well, who could have predicted that?"

"This is Valley Mall?" I ask as we walk through the parking lot. I've been here a zillion times, but it looks so different tonight. Like, shabby. I wonder when they did the remodel.

Mrs. Gray clucks again. "You've never been to this mall before?"

"Is there a Nordstrom's here?"

"Is that the name of a store? It doesn't sound familiar, dear."

It's only my favorite store in the world, I want to shout, *with a shoe sale to die for.*

Speaking of *to die for*, what if I'm dead? Could I have passed out in the bathtub and drowned? Or maybe Mariel got so pissed off, she strangled me.

I bite my lip to test the death theory. It hurts. I guess I'm alive.

"I hate to take advantage," I tell Mrs. Gray, "but could you buy me some makeup?" Tonight's the first time in years I've been in public without it.

"As long as it's tasteful," she says. "There's a drugstore in the mall."

Drugstore makeup is not tasteful. Drugstore makeup is gross. But it's Mrs. Gray's money. "Thanks."

* * *

Once there, she points to a three-pack of eye shadow in turquoise, violet, and powder puff pink.

Even more gross. I don't care what decade it is, I respect my eyelids too much for garish jewel shades. I shake my head.

"How about earth tones then? Not that you need anything on that lovely face of yours."

Lovely face. No one uses the word *lovely* on me. I can't help smiling.

I select a three-pack of shadow: Healthy Tan, Tauperiffic, and Muskrat Love. I also buy a lipstick, blush, eyeliner, and mascara. All that face paint costs less than I spend on a lipstick from MAC back home. Too bad I wasn't beamed to the 70's with my wallet.

Next, Mrs. Gray takes me to May Company, pre-merger with Robinsons. "I saw lovely peasant dresses here last week which I think would be darling on you."

I'd rather stay naked in her bathtub. There is no such thing as a lovely peasant dress. It's a contra . . . contrasomething in terms. Or some other word I think I was supposed to learn in English class last year.

"Where are the jeans?" I ask the salesclerk.

"The Calvin Kleins and Gloria Vanderbilts are right under that disco ball. We don't call them jeans," she scoffs.

Yeah, well, I don't call this a department store, I want to say.

I find Levi's 501s. Thank God some things never change.

Mrs. Gray buys me two pairs. Then she says, "Let's get you some sleepwear and undergarments."

There's that cute word again, *undergarments.*

Mrs. Gray walks to a rack of fluorescent polyester and dull flannel nightgowns.

Not cute at all. My steps slow. This is so not me. I miss Victoria's Secret and thongs. Assuming it's possible to miss something that hasn't been created yet.

I swerve and make a dash for a pair of black, silky pajamas. Mrs. Gray puts a surprisingly strong arm around my shoulder. I can't help flinching. I'm not used to that. At least not from females.

"You're much too sweet for tawdry garments like these." She steers me away from the lingerie, to the granny nightgowns and old lady underwear.

My mom never steered me to anything. Some small part of me likes being called sweet. I could be sweet here. No one here knows I got caught with a bottle of peppermint schnapps and Adam Blaine in the art room at school, or that Mom sent Mariel to the last two back-to-school nights, or that I've never met my father. I could be anything I want here.

Tyler's mom holds a flowery, baby blue flannel nightgown up against my body. "This is perfect for you."

"Me?"

"Yes, dear. You. It's sweet."

Me, Shay Saunders, sweetheart who hangs out with honor students and wears flannel nightgowns. It's tempting.

After Mrs. Gray buys me a lot of "sweet" things, our arms are heavy with bags as we walk to the station wagon together. "Thank you," I tell her, my voice a little shaky. My mom hasn't taken me shopping in years. She keeps me in credit cards, but it's not the same. "I'll try to pay you back, Mrs. Gray." She's been so kind, I even mean it.

"It's the least I can do. Now, let me drive you home."

Gawd! I hadn't thought of that.

"Are you okay, dear? Do you know how to get to your house—er, apartment, from here?"

Stall, I tell myself. "That's nice of you to offer, Mrs. Gray, but I left some of my things at your house."

"I'll swing by so you can run in and get your things, and then I'll take you home. Where do you live? Do you need anything else? Food?"

She is so damn nice, I almost can't lie to her. Almost. "I live in Reseda. I don't need anything, thanks." Except a pint of Ben & Jerry's Phish Food, a place to sleep, and a time machine.

As soon as we get to the house, I race upstairs and fling open Tyler's bedroom door.

He jumps a little. He's at his desk chair with his back to me, craning his neck my way. "You caught me," he says.

Holy crap. I know what teenage boys do in their rooms. "I'm so sorry. It's perfectly normal. I should have knocked."

"Not that normal, actually. There are only four other people in my school with computers."

"Huh?"

"You caught me showing nerd tendencies." He points to his cluttered desk. "I like to take apart my computer, see if I can make it run more efficiently."

"Ohh. I caught you playing with *computer* parts."

His giant monstrosity of a computer barely resembles my laptop. It's about the size of the fridge in my bedroom at home, and looks like a desktop computer got messed up on steroids. The thing is turned backward. Bright wires surround clunky metal. Some of the parts lie scattered on Tyler's desk next to a diagram neatly hand-drawn in various pencil colors.

I can't believe I'm stuck with this guy. Although he probably has a rich future in Silicon Valley. "Your mom wants to drive me home," I say. "And unless her station wagon doubles as a time machine, I don't know what to tell her."

"Hmm." He looks at the Einstein poster over his bed. "What would Albert do?"

"I have no clue, but your mother's waiting downstairs for me."

"Aha! I'll pretend to take you to Reseda, and then you can sneak back in the house later. Let's go talk to my mom."

When Tyler offers to drive me home, Mrs. Gray lifts her eyebrows half an inch, but she says okay.

I can't sleep, and it's not just because Shay is lying in my bed again. I'm trying to process the fact that she's actually from the future. The pope proved it. I have no idea how Shay actually got to 1978 from 2006, and why she ended up *here*. Was it something I did on the computer? The pipes under our bathtub? Is Shay the answer to my prayers?

Ridiculous. There has to be science involved.

I think.

Einstein said science without religion is lame, and religion without science is blind. I have no idea what that means. And I have no idea what Shay is doing here.

I'll probably lie awake half the night trying to figure things out.

I've been lying awake half the night trying to figure things out.

"Can't sleep?" Tyler says at the same time I say, "I can't sleep." It's like we have a karmic connection.

"Want to go outside?" I ask him.

"Now? In the middle of the night?"

"Why not? It could be fun."

"Fun. That's my goal this year." He says it like he's talking about getting A's or learning Latin. "Senior year of high school is supposed to be fun. Wild and crazy fun, not backgammon and computers fun. Yes, Shay, let's sneak out of the house in the middle of the night and have fun."

"Whatever. I just wanted some fresh air."

We head downstairs. Tyler opens the sliding glass door

to the backyard, then points in the faint moonlight to a wooden glider. We sit so close we're touching. "How did you wind up in my bathtub?" he asks me. "I can't believe you're from the future. I mean, I can believe it. When my dad said the pope died, I—"

"You didn't believe me before."

He doesn't answer.

"Your father is really up on the news," I say to change the subject.

"He's well-informed about everything. Politics, the stock market. Everything except his family."

I can't see Tyler's face well, but I hear the hurt in his voice.

"I shouldn't complain," he says. "He works hard to support our family. And it's not as if I come from a broken home. You've never even seen your father. Is it hard?"

I don't answer. No one's ever asked me before. If I tell the truth—that I wonder about my father a lot, what he looks like, if he has other kids, if he ever thinks about me beyond the child support checks—if I tell Tyler that, I might start crying right here, and Tyler would be sorry he ever asked.

But maybe he'd hold me and wipe my tears and say he understood. Or maybe he'd think I was just a stupid, dramatic girl.

"Shay, why did you come here?"

His voice is so gentle. I think he would have understood about my dad.

"I don't know what I'm doing here." Gawd, I sound as soft

as Tyler. That's not me. I'm no wimp. I cross my arms. "I need to get home. I'm having this big blowout eighteenth birthday party in a few weeks. Plus twenty-eight years."

"We can throw you a party here. My mom bakes the best birthday cakes."

"That's not the kind of party I meant. It was going to be a kegger."

"Oh," he says.

"So I have to go home and invite people before they make other plans."

"And I bet a lot of people from home miss you."

"Yeah." Who misses me? Mariel, maybe. Jake's probably weirded out about where I went. Mom might miss me once she notices I'm gone.

Tyler stretches his arm across the glider. It's not around me exactly, but it's behind my back. He clears his throat. "If you're lonely here . . ."

"What?"

He moves his head in close to mine.

"Oh, gawd. You're not making a pass at me, are you?"

"No!" he squeaks, jerking his arm back to his side and leaning away from me. "But did you have to sound so disgusted?"

"I just want to get back to 2006, okay?"

"Maybe we could help you," he says.

"We?"

"My best friend Evie and I. We're taking AP Physics, and Evie scored a perfect 800 on the math SAT."

55

"La di freakin' da."

"At least have lunch with us."

"I'll eat with you if you'll help me."

"Okay. You ready to go to bed?"

What a horndog.

"You know, back to my room. I'll take the floor again."

"Oh. Yeah. Thanks."

People are gawking. Even Evie. Especially Evie. She's sitting on the school bus a row behind Shay and me, but I feel her eyes burning into us through her glasses. Practically everyone on the bus is at least stealing glances. I bet they're looking at Shay, thinking *Wow!* and then looking at me, thinking *Why?*

I return their stares and add a grin. I have replaced the title of Tyler Gray, Unpopular Nerd with Tyler Gray, Foxy Chick Magnet.

"I'm glad you decided to accompany me to school, Shay." I talk loudly to ensure that everyone on the bus can hear me.

"You better honor your end of the deal and get your friend to help me," she says.

I stare out the window. The Valley looks different. We pass orange groves, barren hills, big front yards, and packs of children. There's a dingy diner called Krasno's where my Starbucks is now.

Inside the bus, I'm surrounded by bright eye shadow, white boys with Afros, and huge collars sharp as weapons. Other styles are more familiar—wrap skirts, platform shoes, and dyed blond hair.

"You sure you don't want to go to classes with me?" Tyler asks when the bus stops.

"Totally. I'll see you at lunch." I rush off the bus to check out my school. It's since been renamed for Jerry Brown, who was a mayor or governor or something. The campus itself seems like it's barely changed over the last twenty-eight years, though. The buildings are laid out the same. It's only the students who've changed. Don't they know how awful they look with their big hair and unbuttoned shirts?

Gawd, I sound like an old lady, like my English teacher who's always ranting about hipster jeans. Maybe in twenty-eight years my friends and I will seem ridiculous. Make that fifty-six years, I guess.

After wandering through school, I stand outside my homeroom watching strangers go in. I have no clue what to do next. The bell rings, a kid slams the classroom door, and I bite my lip.

I head toward the 2006 stoner hangout. It beats hanging around talking to air.

I spot a small group of slouching kids. They're in the same spot as the 2006 stoners—in the far left corner of campus, against the back gate. I wonder if there's always a stoner hangout behind every school, throughout time.

A pretty girl can make friends quickly. I approach the group with a smile and an uplifted chest, which unfortunately is locked in the thick cage of a bra Mrs. Gray bought for me. "Hey," I call out to them.

"Hey yourself," a girl mutters before turning her back on me.

Check that—a pretty girl can make *male* friends quickly.

A boy with shoulder-length feathered hair walks over. "What's shakin'?"

"I'm Shay."

"Louis," he says, "but everyone calls me Buzz."

"Let me guess why."

" 'Cause I like catching a buzz." He laughs, a slow chuckle like he's imitating Jeff Spicoli in *Fast Times at Ridgemont High*. I wouldn't be surprised if he got a pizza delivered to his next class. If he shows up to class.

"You're not going to narc on us, are you?" the girl asks.

"I'm no narc. I'm a new student."

"Right on," says a boy with a giant, curly brown Afro. He pulls out a thermos from his lunch box. "You want some?"

"What is it?" I smirk. "Milk?"

"What's the traditional Thanksgiving drink?"

"Yeah, I could use some Wild Turkey."

Smiles all around, at least from the guys.

I take a long swig.

Evie and I are sitting in the corner of the lunch area by ourselves, per usual. But today is different. I'm picking at my food, looking around, checking my watch, hoping that Shay will appear.

Evie keeps asking me questions. "That girl sitting with you on the bus actually slept in your bed the last two nights? She really just showed up in your bathtub? You think she's a runaway? What if she's an escaped prisoner?"

I haven't mentioned the small detail about Shay being from the future. Knowing Evie, with her curious and scientific mind, she'd pepper her with questions until Shay got fed up and found someone else's bed to sleep in.

"Listen." I lean across the table and lower my voice. "I need a big favor."

"Sure. You want help with calculus? Don't be ashamed."

"I need you to pretend you're Shay's mother over the phone."

"What?"

"I have to convince my folks to let Shay live with me."

"You're nuts."

"My mom thinks Shay has terrible parents. If she talks to them, she might let her stay."

"And if your mother finds out it's really me on the phone, I'll get in big trouble. I'm a genius, not an actress."

"Please, Evie."

"No."

"There she is." I nod my head in her direction. "Isn't she pretty? She's going to eat lunch with us. I'm the luckiest guy on this entire planet. The entire solar system. The entire universe of solar systems."

"Exaggerate much, Tyler?"

"I'll pay you. Ten dollars. Think of the *Star Wars* collectibles you can buy with that." I'm talking to Evie but staring at Shay.

"No."

I watch her approach, my neck craned, my face frozen. She's smiling. She has big white teeth, straight as a model orthodontia patient's.

I wave to her, a small acknowledging bobble of my hand. Not in a show-offy way. I hope not, anyway. "Please, Evie. I'd be forever grateful to you. Ten bucks if you'll pretend to be Shay's mother."

She sighs. "Twenty."

"Great! I owe you."

Evie puts out her hand to shake.

"Not now," I whisper. "Shay will see us."

Shay stands right beside me, so close I can smell her. She's got a nasty cigarette odor on her.

"Where have you been?" I ask.

"Killing time."

"Hi," Evie says.

"This is Shay," I say as if Evie doesn't already know all about her. "And this is Evie." I jerk my head in her direction, but keep watching Shay and her smile.

"Nice to meet you, Shay. I'm Evie Justus, Tyler's best and oldest friend. Well, not oldest, but most long lasting."

"So how do I get back?" Shay wobbles forward, then sets her hand on my shoulder to break her fall.

Oh, no. She's drunk again. I can smell the alcohol on her breath.

"Or, like, forward? Twenty-eight years or whatever."

She leans her body into mine. "I need help getting to 2006."

"She's doing a report," I lie. "For school. What if someone visited from the future and wanted to go home again? How would she do it?"

"Now I get it. She just wants the geeks to do her homework," Evie says.

Shay plops down next to me on the bench. "That's, like, not it at all."

"Time travel isn't covered in AP Physics. I can't help you," Evie says.

"You promised, Tyler." Shay's midnight eyes plead with mine. "At's the whole reason I'm at school today. You told me your friend was smart."

"You promised her I'd help her with her report?" Evie asks. "You just assumed I'd do it?"

I'd like to respond, but can't because Shay's knee is now touching my thigh and freezing my brain.

To make matters worse, or better, actually, she puts her hand on my thigh. "Please, please, peas. I mean *please*," she says. "Someone, like, just get me out of here."

Cool as Antarctica, Evie says, "Just go over to that table where you belong and you'll be fine." She points to the popular table. Rick The Dick is pinching Loose Lori's ass, and a trio of skinny blondes are sharing a brownie.

Man, I wish I were sitting there. "Evie, she just wants to know about time travel."

"She's bad news. I think she may have been drinking,

possibly. Ten seconds after we help with her report, she'll ditch us for the popular kids and laugh when they trip us in the hall."

"What's wrong with popular people?" Shay asks.

"Nothing. And we're plenty popular, anyway," I lie. To impress Shay, I wave in the direction of the popular kids. They'll never notice me, anyway.

Oops. Mr. Popular himself, Rick The Dick, glares at me. He stands up and swaggers toward us.

Is waving at someone out of your popularity league grounds for getting beat up? I look around for a weapon, or better yet, a lunch monitor.

The Dick stops at our table. He smiles.

Maybe Shay's my ticket to popularity. Being seen with a beautiful girl like her has to raise a guy's social standing. I return The Dick's smile.

He leans his face right into Shay's. "You, foxy lady, must be new. Because if I ever saw you before, I'd totally remember."

She gives him a smile approximately seventy-five percent bigger than the one she gave us.

"Let me show you around." He puts his oafish hand on her arm.

She doesn't move his hand away. She does move her hand off my thigh.

"Tell me, are you a strong swimmer?" The Dick asks her.

"I can swim. Why?"

"In case I need rescuing. I'm drowning in your eyes."

I groan.

Shay's smile grows even bigger.

I summon up a half ounce of courage and point out, in a tone that's hopefully reasonable enough not to earn a punch from The Dick, "Shay, I thought you wanted us to help you at lunchtime today."

"Tomorrow, 'kay?" she says before going off with The Dick. For a tour of the school, and God knows what else.

Only two things are infinite—the universe and human stupidity. Albert Einstein.

Rick's at least six feet tall, with thick blond hair, intense blue eyes, and a build like a bank vault. The way he touches my arm, so sure, so manly, makes up for his half-unbuttoned shirt displaying a mass of corn-colored chest hairs.

"You dig?"

Gawd, I must have been staring.

He doesn't wait for an answer. He undoes another button on his shirt like a male stripper. I try hard not to shout *Stop!*

As we walk through the cafeteria, a lot of people say hi to him. He gives all of them shout-outs in return, not just the jockish guys and pretty girls, but a fat boy and a pimply girl too. Is that a 70's thing or a Rick thing? Whatever it is, it's nice.

"So what's a gorgeous chick like you doing here?" he asks me.

I give him my shrug that shows off my chest.

We pass by the bungalows. Twenty-eight years later, our school still has them. Then we walk through the vacant baseball field. I don't see Professional Tour Guide as Rick's future career, given that he hasn't said a word about the school since we started the "tour." Not that I expected one.

He stops at the bleachers, takes my hand, and leads me to a top row seat.

I smile at him. "Hey."

He stares into my eyes. "Where have you been hiding all this time?"

I look away. "Just, um, Reseda."

"Why did you transfer to our school?"

"To find a cute guy like you."

He laughs. "No, really. Why?"

What is he, a private eye? To shut him up, I put my hands on his cheeks and move my face close to his. He has a tough-guy jaw, short, golden stubble, and rugged but unblemished skin.

"What school were you at before?"

I kiss him, hard, and he stops asking questions.

11

Shay Saunders is (1) gorgeous, (2) sexy, and (3) a whiner. She's sitting next to me on the school bus, rolling her eyes and/or sighing and/or muttering "I hate this" every time there's a stop. "I can't believe you don't have your own car," she says. "How are you going to get any girls?"

"As if that's all that's stopping me."

"I wouldn't be so shallow as to choose a boyfriend based on his mode of transportation," Evie says from across the aisle.

Since when is Evie interested in boyfriends? The only guys she's ever seemed excited about are Jonas Salk and J. D. Salinger.

Shay turns toward Evie. "You're in L.A., where cars are king and people are shallow."

"You're a good example of that," Evie says. "Blowing us off the minute a foxy guy comes by."

Evie thinks The Dick is foxy? I thought she was too busy calculating people's IQs to notice what they looked like.

"Shay, if you want our help, try treating us with respect," Evie tells her.

"And maybe you can find a way to help us too," I add.

"I got it." Shay snaps her fingers. Her nails are painted gray-blue. Very strange. Maybe weird nails are in style in the future. "We'll do, like, *Extreme Makeover*," she says. "Not that extreme though. More like a *Queer Eye for the Straight Guy* kind of thing."

"What?" Evie and I both ask.

"I'll give you makeovers."

"I don't want a makeover," Evie says. "I'm fine with my low social status. I don't need to talk to ditzy cheerleaders and brutes like Rick The Dick. Actually, I enjoy just being around Tyler and having intelligent conversations."

I raise my hand. "Actually, I would like to talk to ditzy cheerleaders."

"Good. Here's your first lesson. Don't ever raise your hand. Not even in class. And never say *actually*. It reeks geekspeak," she says. "So you're in?"

"No way, José," Evie says.

"Tyler, please let me do you over," Shay purrs.

When a beautiful girl sits next to you and begs to "do you over," with her soft voice and pouty lips and long-lashed eyes, there's only one response. I nod my head up and down and say, "Do me over!"

"Just make sure you help me with the time-travel stuff," Shay adds.

"I've already been working on it. This morning in physics class I came up with an idea. We could experiment with it today."

"Great!" Evie exclaims. "Science experiments are

right up my alley. I'll get off the bus with you and lend a hand."

"Great," I say without enthusiasm.

We all walk to my house, tell Mom we're working on a physics class project, and retreat to the garage. I take out the Christmas lights and wind a long string of them around Shay's arm.

"This can't possibly work," Evie says.

I sure hope not. There's no way I want to return Shay to the future. "Evie, you know time travel has to reach the speed of light."

"The speed of *light*, not light *bulbs*. Einstein's constant *C*, the speed of light, is measured in a vacuum, not by how fast a string of Christmas bulbs lights up. Jeez, Tyler, that's just basic physics."

Physics, shmysics. I'm touching a gorgeous girl. Okay, so I'd rather be kissing her than stringing lights around her, but, still.

"Hurry up!" Shay says.

Oops. I've lingered on her arm. And I think I'm grinning. It's Christmas in September. "Do you want me to be fast or accurate?"

"Fast."

Darn. I was aiming for slow and sensual. I finish wrapping her arms, but pause once I get to her chest, her soft, generous chest.

"Want me to take a turn?" Evie asks.

"No!" I wind the lights down Shay's body. Was there ever a more perfect behind? I doubt it.

"Are you almost finished?" Shay asks.

I get to say something I've only ever dreamed of: "Spread your legs."

And she does, and I'm wrapping the string of Christmas lights all over the world's second most shapely legs, the first being Lynda Carter's from *Wonder Woman*. Shay's legs are a very close second place.

"Are you *done*?"

"I guess."

"Let's try it already. I have a birthday party to plan back home."

"Here goes nothing." Evie plugs in the lights.

"Ow!" Shay screams. "You're burning me! Turn that off!"

Evie pulls the plug out of the wall and says, "I told you it wouldn't work."

"Look what you did!" Shay holds up her arm. I peer at it, but the only damage I see is a few singed arm hairs. "You maimed me!" Shay says. "Take these stupid lights off me."

"I'm sorry." I pounce on her leg.

"Gawd. Get away." She gives me a small kick as if I'm a dog in heat. "I'll do it myself." She twists and turns to unwind the string of bulbs from her body. Then she tosses the lights back in their box. "I can't believe you burned my arm."

"I singed it, at most. But I apologize. I didn't know what would happen."

"You didn't really expect Shay to travel in time, though,"

Evie says. Sometimes I wish she weren't so darn smart. She opens the garage door.

"Where are you going?" I ask her.

She walks outside without answering or even turning her head.

"Good-bye, Evie," I say, but I'm not sure she can still hear me.

12

"*I can't believe I'm* still stuck here," Shay says as we stand in the garage.

"I'm sorry."

"Stuck here with you."

"Maybe you should give me that makeover you mentioned."

"You want me to help you now, after you burned my arm?"

"Singed a few arm hairs, you mean. I didn't know that would happen. Shay, please help me be less geeky. This is my last year of high school, my last chance to get invited to the cool parties and stuff, and you may be my last hope." I cock my head and stare at her wide-eyed in an attempt to look especially pitiful. "Please? And afterward, I'll ask my parents to let you stay here."

"Like I have anywhere else to go." She sighs. "Fine, I'll give you a makeover."

"Tyler Gray, reporting for duty, ma'am." I cleverly salute her.

"The military thing? Very uncool." She opens the door connecting the garage to the house and walks in. I drop my hand and follow her.

She leads me to the downstairs bathroom, in front of the mirror, and stands behind me with her silky hands on my cheeks. She has the sweetest scent, like roses sprinkled with cinnamon. I'm loving this makeover already.

"Tyler," Shay says. "Find me some tweezers for your unibrow and an ice cube to numb you. And a scarf or something we can tie over your mouth to muzzle your screams."

"Screams?" I squeak.

She laughs, evilly. "After what you just did to my arm, it's payback time."

"On second thought, maybe I don't need a makeover."

"Take it like a man."

After I give her the instruments of torture, she brings the sharp tweezers dangerously close to my corneas and pulls out one of my eyebrow hairs.

"Ow!"

Her response is to pluck off another hair by its extremely sensitive root.

"Shay, it hurts! Stop! I beg you."

"Quit whimpering." She keeps the tweezers in play. "There's a whole hair forest growing between your eyes."

"I'm sorry about singeing your—ow!—arm. Truce! You're torturing me!"

She waves the tweezers in front of my face. "Keep your eyes closed, shut up, and hold still, if you know what's good for you."

So I do. I grit my teeth too. I think I hear Shay laughing behind me. It's all an excruciatingly agonizing blur.

Finally, she says, "Not bad. The redness and swelling shouldn't last long."

"Redness and swelling?"

"Open your eyes and look in the mirror," Shay orders.

Whoa. She was right about the brow tweeze making a difference. It's almost worth the horrific pain. My eyes look bigger and brighter. Which I don't admit, because a guy's not supposed to care about that stuff.

"Do you have a Dustbuster for your old unibrow hairs?" Shay asks me.

"Huh?"

"Dirt Devil?"

I stare at her.

"Swiffer?"

"I'll get a broom."

"Fine. I'm exhausted."

"*You're* exhausted?" I raise my skimpy brows. "I just had practically half my face torn off."

"Well, I just suffered fourth-degree arm burns," Shay says. "I'm going to sit on that glider in the backyard."

"Want company?"

"No! Just clean up in here and then go ask your mother to let me stay. And keep those damn Christmas lights away from me." She exits the bathroom, closing the door behind her.

I stare at myself again in the mirror. I must admit I look kind of cute.

After I rid the bathroom of plucked brow hairs, I use the upstairs phone to call Evie.

She's cranky. "What was that all about in your garage? Tyler, you know Christmas lights aren't going to send anyone into the future."

I smile. "That was all about wrapping a string of lights around a pair of long, shapely legs."

"Shay's more than just a pair of legs, Tyler."

"I know you're above thinking about stuff like that, Evie, but—"

"How do you know what I'm above thinking about?"

"Whoa. Mellow out, Evie."

"You're so preoccupied with—"

"Hey, listen. I'm going to talk to my mom now about letting Shay live with us. I'll try to have her call you. So wait by the phone, okay? And get ready to disguise your voice and act like a terrible parent."

"Now?" Evie sounds even crankier.

"I promise to give you twenty dollars if it works. I was saving for upgraded computer parts, but that's all right."

"I can't believe I'm helping you get together with a girl."

"Yeah, you're a good friend. Thanks a lot." I hang up the phone and look for Mom.

She's in the kitchen as usual. While she makes cookies, I sit at the table giving myself a pep talk. *You can pull this off, Tyler. It's just a little lie. Shay is counting on you.* Finally, I say, "My friend Shay is in really bad shape. Could she stay with us for a while? Temporarily, of course."

Mom looks up from the mixing bowl. "I feel bad for her, but I'm not her mother."

"Her mother isn't acting like one." I point to the kitchen phone. "Call her and ask."

"No, Tyler."

"She'll just be here for a little while, until things get straightened out. She can live with her aunt as soon as she returns from France."

"No."

"Mom, she hardly has any food."

"She's welcome to stay for dinner tonight."

"She's so lonely living by herself. Please, Mom. Call her parents. Can I dial the number for you?"

She gets an egg from the refrigerator, cracks it open, stirs it into the batter, and tastes the cookie dough on the spoon. She nods. Which probably means she's satisfied with the batter, but could be interpreted as *Yes, Tyler, you can call Shay's parents.*

I pick the latter, wasting no time in dialing Evie's number and putting the handset to Mom's ear. I hope Evie's standing by. Mom mouths *no,* but I keep the phone where it is.

She wipes her hands on the apron and holds the handset to her ear. "Hello. Is this Mrs. Saunders?" Pause. "Mrs. Saunders, I'm calling about your daughter."

Phew.

Evie is a duchess of deception, a manure magician, a true b.s. artist. After a few minutes, she has Mom swiping at her eyes and saying, "But she's your own child," and, "Don't you care what happens to her?" and, "I'd be happy to have her." Evie definitely deserves the twenty dollars I promised her, as well as my undying friendship.

Finally, Mom slams down the phone. "Shay can stay. She can sleep in Heather's room."

I hug her, trying not to whoop for joy.

"And I'm calling the child welfare office."

"No, Mom!"

"That woman should be reported!"

"Just wait. Please. Shay's aunt will take her in."

"All right. But now how am I going to break this news to your father?" Mom says.

The better question is whether he'll even notice. "Will Dad be home tonight?"

"Yes. That'll be two nights in a row."

I never catch a break.

After Tyler gives me the thumbs-up, I walk into the kitchen to thank his mother.

Ouch. She's wearing green eye shadow, bright orange lipstick, and a pink polyester dress. Which is enough to give someone a headache, or if someone already had a headache from a Wild Turkey–fest seven hours ago, make it a lot worse.

"Oh, shoot, I think I missed a wrinkle when I ironed this." She's staring down at the skirt of her frilly lilac apron.

The woman irons her aprons? Is she insane? My mom doesn't even own an apron.

"Shay, sweetheart, can you tie this for me?" She motions to the apron strings dangling by her legs.

I'll help anyone who calls me a sweetheart. As I tie her apron, she says, "And could you help me fix dinner?"

"I didn't know dinner was broken."

She doesn't laugh.

"That's a joke, Mrs. Gray. I'm happy to help."

"Oh, sorry. Ha ha, good one," she says somberly.

She's a sweetheart herself, though her makeup job could scare small children. And there's something nice, in a dorky way, about preparing a family meal.

Except for the raw chicken. She shows me how to remove the gizzards, which are another name for the disgusting parts. There's a scrawny, raw neck made up of thick skin and tiny bones, a black stinky liver, and a rubbery thing which I don't even want to know what it is. The gizzards are even grosser than regular raw chicken. Like *Fear Factor* gross. But I take them out for Mrs. Gray, trying not to breathe through my nose.

I tear off iceberg lettuce so she can rinse the leaves and put them in a bowl she cranks called a salad spinner. "One of these days," I tell her over the whirring noise, "the market will sell lettuce already washed, torn, and bagged, and chicken already cut up."

"People appreciate a home-cooked meal."

I nod. They do appreciate it. I do, at least.

Mom and I never cook. We order takeout from China Express, Salad Shoppe, or California Quickie, or we microwave Lean Cuisines, and we watch *E!* or *Extra* while we eat. Once Mariel tried to bake cookies with me, but Mom yelled at her later for bringing sweets into the house. Mom doesn't trust the housekeepers' cooking. "Those Mexicans put lard in everything. That's why they're so fat," she says. She doesn't get, or doesn't care, that none of the housekeepers was really fat. They just weren't L.A. thin.

After Mrs. Gray and I finish making the chicken and salad, we "fix" scalloped potatoes, lima beans, and rice pudding.

"You don't need to go to extra trouble for me," I tell her.

She stirs the rice pudding while opening the oven to check on the potatoes. "Oh, this is normal."

"We never cook in my house."

Mrs. Gray claps her hand over her mouth.

I hope she doesn't get that Day-Glo orange lipcrap on her teeth. It looks like it might be poisonous. I imagine what she's thinking: *Even worse than Shay's parents abandoning her, the poor child didn't get home-cooked meals.*

I'm chopping bananas and Mrs. Gray is dissolving lime Jell-O powder into hot water when the phone rings. On her way to answer it, she primps her permed hair as if the caller could see her.

After a few moments of chitchat, there's a long silence. Mrs. Gray's forehead is all wrinkled.

Uh-oh.

"But I'm making that Jell-O mold you like so much," she says softly.

Pause.

"Yes." She sighs. "A big client."

Pause.

"Of course I understand."

She hangs up the telephone, freezes for a moment, then pours the bowl of watery Jell-O into the sink. She gathers the canned pineapple rings, maraschino cherries, and mini marshmallows, and shoves them into the cupboard. "Who wants to eat with boring old me?" She closes the cupboard door with a bang.

"I do, Mrs. Gray. Not that you're boring. Or old."

"What if I bought short skirts? Like you wear. Like those women's libbers in miniskirts and no bras."

I'm not making her over. I'll have my hands full with Tyler. Besides, putting Mrs. Gray in tight sweaters won't solve her problems. Though I wish she'd ditch the church lady dresses and bright eye shadow. *Not my business.* "Mrs. Gray, you look just fine."

She flips her apron up and buries her face in it. In a muffled voice, she says, "I feel so stuck."

She's stuck in the 70's as much as I am. I have to help her. "You could get a job. You seem to be a hard worker." What an understatement. She makes Martha Stewart look like a soap opera addict.

Of course! She could be the next Martha Stewart. Or rather the pre–Martha Stewart. "Mrs. Gray. You could, like, start a TV show with household hints."

She takes her face out of the apron. "Like Heloise?"

"Sure." Never heard of her, but I'll go with it. "Like, with tips about cooking and flower arranging and stuff, advice about making everything just right at home. You could start your own magazine, and, oh my gawd, next thing you know you'd be worth millions. Only don't sell stock with insider information, okay?"

"What?"

"Mom, are you all right?" Tyler stands just outside the kitchen.

"Of course." She has a pained look on her face. But that seems to be her usual expression.

"When's dinner?" he asks.

"Dinner? Right. I guess we could eat now."

Heather comes down and we set the table. While we eat, Mrs. Gray serves herself small helpings, pushes them around on her plate, gets up to offer us more food, steals occasional glances at the phone, and doesn't eat a thing. Finally, she says, "I can't get a job, Shay. I'm a wife, a mother."

"Oh, sure you can. Tyler and Heather are in school all day anyway. I could help you find a job."

"My husband wouldn't want me to work."

"What do *you* want?"

"She wants what Dad wants. She wants to make him happy." Tyler clenches his fork in his fist. "We're supposed to be a happy family."

Mrs. Gray gets up from the table, taking her plate toward the kitchen. "Girls, can you clean up after dinner?" Her voice wobbles. "I'm going to rest in my room."

"Mom?" Tyler says.

"Are you okay?" Heather asks.

"I'm fine." But she sounds even more miserable than usual.

"See what you did?" Tyler spits out.

"Me? What *I* did? You know, with your attitude toward women, you wouldn't last a day in 2006."

"I don't need to. It's 1978." He gets up from the table.

"At least clear your plate," I tell him.

"That's women's work."

I follow him as he heads for the stairs. "Are you telling me when your genius friend Evie grows up, she's not allowed to be a physicsologist or whatever?"

He turns around. "Physicist, Shay. Sheesh. And Evie's not really a girl. I mean, I don't think of her that way."

"News flash, Tyler. Evie's a girl. And she should be allowed to do whatever she wants. Just like your mother. Gawd."

We don't speak for the rest of the evening. The only person I talk to is Heather as we clean in the kitchen, and that's just to say things like, "Can this go in the dishwasher?" and "Which sponge should I use?"

Later, I lie in the trundle bed in her room, listening to her steady breaths while I struggle for sleep.

I picture my bedroom at home. I miss my things. My laptop, my cell phone, my mini fridge. I hope someone's watering my fern. Probably Mariel is, if my mom hasn't fired her yet.

I try to conjure up Mom's thin face, her eyes, lighter than mine and narrower. Supposedly, my dad is a dark-eyed, married millionaire. Mom met him in a hotel bar. We get big checks from Texas every month. Mom says they'll stop when I turn eighteen, so that's why she still hangs out in bars. I imagine my mother's hair, dyed sunkissed blond and lengthened and thickened with $1,500 extensions, the butt she firms with *Buns of Steel* workouts four times a week, her stiletto heels, which she walks on like they're sneakers, her weak warning of "Don't do anything I wouldn't do," which leaves my options wide open, as she rushes out the door.

I let out a little moan. Gawd, I hope Heather's asleep.

"Shay?"

I never catch a break.

"Are you okay?"

I switch my thoughts from Mom to happier ones. I picture the bent back of Mrs. Gray, her ruffled apron with its thick bow that I tied for her today. "I'm fine, Heather."

"I want to say I'm sorry. For calling you Shake, and stuff like that."

"It's okay. Thanks for sharing your room." I picture Heather now, her scraggly hair and pale, angry face. "I was watching you tonight, Heather. You'd look great in bright colors, especially near your face. Something with a red collar, or maybe, like, a turquoise scarf."

"You have a problem with my clothes?"

"No, but you could do even better." I know I sound fake as hell. "I could show you makeup tricks too."

"I'm going back to sleep."

"Okay," I whisper. But I've ruined the moment. It's not okay. Nothing's okay.

13

"I can't stand riding this bus," Shay says. "You have to get me home."

"Why should I help you? You complain about the school bus like you're better than everyone else. You tell my mother she should get a job even though my dad doesn't want her to. You promise me a makeover, but all you do is pull out half my eyebrows—in a highly painful manner, I might add."

"Gawd. And you say *I* complain a lot. What the hell do you want from me?"

"For one thing, you can help me figure out this time travel stuff."

She looks at me like I'm nuts. "How am I going to do that? In case you haven't noticed, I'm not an honors student like you."

"I don't know if you can help, but you can at least try. Two heads are better than one. Three, actually, if Evie works with us too. And you're the only one who actually experienced time travel. Maybe you can remember some clues about how it happened."

"I was passed out, Tyler." The bus stops a little short at a red light, and Shay slams her hands into the seatback in front of her. "Plus, I don't know anything about science."

"Attend classes with me. My physics class might be especially useful."

"Even if I wanted to enroll in your school—which I don't—it's not like I have transcripts or a birth certificate. Technically, I haven't even been born yet."

"You could go to the school library and read books."

She shakes her head. "I don't do books. I take it there's no Net hookup at the library?"

"What do you need a net for?"

"*The* Net, not *a* net. Never mind."

"So is it a deal?"

She rolls her eyes. "Okay. I'll try to learn something."

"And you'll give me a makeover, try making me popular."

"Deal."

"Deal." I offer my hand to shake, but she rolls her eyes again.

I fumble through my backpack propped between my feet and pick out *The Great Gatsby*. "Since I'm going to be spending a lot of time researching time travel theories, why don't you read this and explain it to me. English is actually my weak subject."

"Everything is my weak subject."

"Not romance, I bet. I don't get the romance."

"No, you probably wouldn't." She takes the book.

She comes to our table at lunchtime with a whole pile of books. Besides *The Great Gatsby*, there are two beauty and fashion volumes and a physics text. Maybe she *has* been reading about time travel. I make room for her beside me.

She hides the books under the table and sits down. "I've figured out hem lengths and makeup trends for the year 1978," she announces like it's Nobel Prize–worthy.

"Shay, you have a library card?"

"I don't need one. I guess barcodes haven't been invented yet."

"Barcodes? Huh?"

"I'll bring the books back when I'm done with them," she says. "Hey, there's nothing faster than the speed of light, right?"

Across from us, Evie says, "You read that correctly, Shay. Nothing can surpass the speed of light."

She quizzes us more, about jet propulsion and the fourth dimension. She borrows my notebook and jots down notes.

"See? Physics can be fun," I say.

She rolls her eyes, then claps her hands. "Social makeover time. Tyler, you said physics class can be fun. Don't ever mention that in public again. It's on my list of things a high school student should never say. Listen up."

"This might interest someone who cared about being popular," Evie says.

"Like me." I take a big bite of my bologna sandwich.

Shay clears her throat. "The list of what not to say: One, I like my classes. Two, my parents are cool. Three, I'm not into music. Four, I can't go because I have to study. And five, personality is more important than looks. Got it?" She doesn't wait for a response. "And don't gobble down your food like that, Tyler. It's disgusting."

I swallow the sandwich remnants.

"What if you actually like your classes?" Evie asks.

"Don't use the word *actually*. Reeks of geek."

I open the bag of M&Ms I bought from the school vending machine. "Thanks, Shay."

"My classes are more important to me than popularity," Evie says. "Actually."

Shay takes a few M&Ms. "What if I allow you to say you like one class?"

"*Allow* us? Who died and left you queen?" Evie says.

"You're allowed to like shop class."

"The only class I ever liked was shop class," I say in a fake, deep voice.

"Good!" Shay exclaims.

Across the table, Evie shakes her head. "You hated shop class. You said those two enormous wrestlers kept threatening to stuff you in a wood chipper."

Shay pours out a handful of M&Ms. "I loved shop class."

"A girl taking shop class? What school let you do that?" Evie asks. "You mean you worked with saws and welding equipment and such?"

"Don't say *and such*. Dweeb City," Shay tells her.

"Hey, foxy lady."

Ugh. The Dick has arrived. I can't help stretching my

neck up and around so I can glare at him. He's snuck up behind us, mashing himself against Shay's back like a sex-crazed dog while his arms dangle near her breasts.

Instead of taking mace out of her purse and dousing him with it, like any sane, self-respecting girl would do, she turns her head and grins. "Hi, handsome."

"What are you doing at the dork table?"

"Don't say that," Shay says weakly before putting more of my M&Ms in her mouth.

Sensible person that I am, who knows the minuscule odds of winning a fight against someone (1) taller, (2) heavier, and (3) meaner than me, I look the other way.

"Let's blow this Popsicle joint," The Dick says.

"What?" Shay asks.

"Come with me."

I assume he's asking Shay, not me or Evie. Behind me, he's making some kind of kissing or sucking noise. He must be doing something to Shay's neck.

What is he doing exactly? Slurping it? I mime sticking a finger down my throat.

Evie mumbles, "Dickhead."

"Say what?" The Dick stops the vacuum action long enough to ask.

I clear my throat. "Shay is my friend. Treat her with respect."

The Dick claps his huge hand on my shoulder, like a jungle cat swatting a paw at its prey. I hope that after I'm gone, Shay will appreciate me sacrificing my life for her honor.

He takes his hand off my shoulder and into my bag of M&Ms. "Of course I respect your friend, man."

"Rick, let's take that walk." Shay fishes out another handful of candy.

After they leave, with The Dick's massive arm around Shay's thin shoulders, I can't finish my lunch. Not even my one remaining M&M.

Rick steers me toward the popular table and introduces me around. There's Laura, Lori, Lisa, Debby with a y, Debbie P., and Debbie M., along with John, Jeff, Jack, and Mike.

Despite their feathered hair, supersized collars, and love affair with the word "bitchin'," the girls are a lot like my 2006 friends. They giggle, flip their hair, and suck in their stomachs. The boys have girly, blow-dried locks and big combs which jut out of their back pockets like penis symbols. But they seem familiar too. They still stare at the girls' chests and talk about football and parties. No one's defending their parents' crappy marriage, or asking me to study physics, or giving me books to read.

I play with Rick's chest hairs. "Thanks for letting me meet your friends."

"Thanks for sitting with me." He puts his big hand on my knee. "John's having a bitchin' party Saturday night. Everyone's going. You want to come?"

"Yes," I tell him. "Yes, I totally want to come."

* * *

After lunch I have over two hours to kill. I grab the best book I have, *The Great Gatsby,* and walk to the diner I saw out the school bus window. It's a few blocks away and it looks like a dive, but I'm dying for coffee.

Krasno's Diner is just as dirty on the inside as on the outside, and that's saying a lot. The cheap paintings on the walls need dusting, the floors need washing, the fake plants need a trip to the Dumpster, half the booths need bussing, and the counter needs wiping down.

I walk to the back of the diner and sit on faded, cracked vinyl in a booth that smells like mildew. I wait a long time until a fat guy waddles in from the kitchen.

"Do you serve lattes here, by any chance?"

He scowls. "What? We serve anyone with a shirt, shoes, and cash."

"Never mind. A cup of coffee, please."

He shakes his head and disappears into the kitchen.

I sit there, like, forever, but that's all right. I have nowhere to go, a surprisingly interesting old novel to read, and only seven dollars left from Tyler's stash. What am I going to do for money now?

Duh. It hits me like a slap on the ass. I'll get a job. I never had one before, but so what? I never touched chicken gizzards before either, or wore thrift store clothes, or hung with an honors student.

When the fat guy finally brings my coffee, which tastes like crap, I ask if they're hiring.

He looks me up and down. "*You* want to work *here*?"

I point to the balled-up napkins and dirty plates on the tables. "You could use my help."

"Yeah, all right."

He doesn't even ask for ID. I have to fill out a form. I don't remember my Social Security and driver's license numbers or Tyler's phone number, so I make all of them up.

I can start right away. Bussing tables and washing dishes. Gross.

When I come home from school with Shay and Evie, pull all the magnets off the fridge, and say, "Physics experiment," Mom's eyebrows don't even move a millimeter. I might not be improving in physics, but I'm getting to be a much better liar.

Once we're in the garage, I tell Shay, "I'll try to be gentle with the tape."

"I'll put the magnets on myself," she says.

I'm one step ahead of her. "But what about those hard-to-reach spots, like your back?"

"Okay, but I'll kick your ass if I get hurt again."

I tape the magnets on Shay's soft, smooth, perfect back. I close my eyes and relish the moment.

"Aren't you done yet?" Shay asks.

"He's done," Evie says. "Now what?"

I haven't a clue. Why is Evie insisting on accompanying me for this experiment?

"You want Shay to lean into the station wagon to attempt super-magnetic conduction, right?"

Oh, that's why Evie's here. She's a science whiz. "Super-magnetic conduction. Right."

Shay presses her body into Mom's car. The super-magnetic conduction doesn't work, of course. She scowls at me. "You're no help at all. The only things that have traveled in your stupid experiments are your hands over my body."

"Sorry. I thought the electromagnetic waves—"

"What the hell are those?"

"Come to my physics class and find out."

She untapes the magnets from her arms and throws them on the garage floor. "I told you I'm too dumb for this stuff."

"I don't think so at all," I say.

"I don't get that electric magnet wave thing you and Evie were talking about." She puts her hand under her T-shirt and removes the magnets from her stomach. "Do you mean, like, waves in people's hair or ocean waves or what?"

"Ocean waves. Eureka! Wave simulation in a bathtub!" Tidal forces, ocean waves, could be replicated in a bathtub, generating a whirlpool faster than the speed of light. That must be how Shay got here. I could try to rig a bathroom fan to imitate tidal waves.

"What about ocean waves?" She reaches under her shirt to untape a magnet from her breast.

Wait, Tyler. Do you actually want to send Shay home?

"Tyler, are you thinking of producing a simulation of tidal forces in a bathtub?" Evie asks.

Shay takes the magnets off her long legs. "Tidal forces?" she asks.

"We should work on that idea," Evie says.

*What if the fan actually works, and Shay leaves? You'll
probably never again have such close proximity to a beautiful girl, Tyler. Plus, she promised to help you become popular. Keep Shay here, Tyler, and happy. Keep her mind off
going home.*

"Yeah," Shay says. "Work on that tidal forces idea soon,
before my birthday. I've got a party to plan."

Suddenly it hits me. "How about we throw you a
birthday party, Shay? You could invite your new, popular friends."

"I don't plan to be here on my birthday," she says.

"I know, but just in case."

"A keg party, right? Not, like, a pin-the-tail-on-the-
donkey thing."

"Of course." I say this with no idea how I can even buy
a keg or what one actually looks like. But at least it might
get Shay's mind off of returning home. For now.

15

I'm a $2.30 an hour slave, and I look like it. The fat owner of the diner gave me an ugly white apron with a million stains, a rip, and a hole. Mrs. Gray would be shocked.

As I'm wiping a glob of syrup off a booth and hoping my nails won't break, Mariel shows up at the restaurant. I mean, a younger Mariel, how she looked twenty-eight years ago, which is now. But it's her. Our housekeeper. Or future one, I guess. Whatever. She's still short and chubby, and still moves slowly, with her head down. She walks into the kitchen.

What the hell? I stand nearly frozen, leaning against the table and clenching the wet, soapy cloth. Has Mariel come to take me home? Did she figure out the time travel thing? Or did she get stuck in 1978 too? She's gotten younger here while I'm still seventeen. I can't understand it. Of all the people I know in 2006, why is our housekeeper here?

I leave my rag on the skeezy table and follow her into the kitchen. "Mariel?"

She turns around with a puzzled expression and asks who I am, in Spanish.

My heart sinks. I always thought that was just an expression, but it really does sink, at least an inch, enough to hurt inside my chest. "It's me. Shay. Shay Saunders."

She gives me a thin, polite smile.

I don't go into the *Back to the Future* story. She obviously wouldn't believe it. Instead, I tell her in Spanish that I heard there was a girl named Mariel working here.

She shakes my hand. She hasn't tattooed her wrist yet with that tacky dragonfly.

I should warn her not to do it.

No. She wouldn't listen to me.

"Why aren't you cleaning?" the fat guy yells, so I shuffle out of the kitchen.

Just my luck. Mariel, the only person I know in 1978 and the only one who cares about me in 2006, has no clue who I am.

After dinner, Shay runs into my room. "Your mom's at the market with Heather. I forgot to ask if we have a curfew. I don't want to upset your parents."

I can't help staring at her. I think she's wearing one of Heather's dresses, but it's hardly recognizable now. It's low-cut and a lot shorter. I point to it. "You know how to sew?"

"Are you kidding? Not me. But I'm okay with scissors and duct tape. I call this the Nasty Heidi look."

"Wow," I say like the dork I am.

She laughs. "You know, without the unibrow your eyes seem a lot bigger. Once you get a haircut, I bet you'll look halfway decent."

"Thanks, I guess. Wow."

"You like?" She angles back her shoulders. "So what time's your curfew?"

"Oh, right." I turn to my desk, which has computer parts splayed across it. "The subject of a curfew hasn't really come up. I've never actually stayed out that late."

She shakes her head. "You need a social life like Michael Jackson needs therapy. Like I need a beer." She heads toward the door. "Later."

"Where are you going?"

She turns her head and gives me a smoldering look. "To a party, a keg party."

"I'll come with you, okay? You're supposed to help make me popular."

"Sorry. I'm going as Rick Bowden's date."

The Dick. My leg starts shaking. "Does Heather know you did that to her dress? That was her dress, right?"

"Don't wait up." She leaves without looking back.

I slam my hand on the desk.

Ow. That was stupid of me.

The phone rings, so I rush to the hallway to answer it. "Hello."

"Hi, it's me."

"Evie. Hey. I was just contemplating finding a bridge to jump off. Because guess where Shay just went? To a party with Rick The Dick. She's been here a few weeks and she's already hanging out with the popular people, including my worst enemy. Can you believe it? You and I are in our third year at this school and we've never been to one of those parties."

"What about my shindig last year?" Evie asks.

"The astronomy party to watch the solar eclipse? That was fun. But, no offense, Evie, it wasn't like sharing a keg with the cheerleaders."

"So let's have our own fun. I was actually calling to see if you wanted to go somewhere tonight. Maybe get a slice of pie at Sambos, or see *Star Wars* again."

"We've seen *Star Wars* six times." I let out a sigh. "Thanks for asking, but I'd just be in a bad mood all night, thinking about Shay and The Dick."

"You're always thinking about Shay and The Dick these days."

"I know. You should have seen what she's wearing tonight. Barely anything. She was practically falling out of her—"

"Spare me the details, all right, Tyler?"

"Sorry. Sometimes I forget you're a girl."

There's silence on her end.

"Evie?"

"I'd better get off the phone."

"Okay. I shouldn't go out, anyway. I have a haircut appointment early tomorrow morning at this ritzy salon Shay says the popular people recommended. I'm supposed to ask for the Shaun Cassidy look. I'm paying for it myself because it costs three times as much as Supercuts."

"What would you think if I got a haircut?" Evie asks. "Maybe feathered bangs."

"You? I thought you don't care about your looks."

She doesn't respond.

"Evie? You still there?"

"Yeah. All right, bye." She hangs up the phone.

I'm in a better mood already. Talking to Evie helped, as did thinking about my haircut tomorrow morning. Plus, Shay promised to take me shopping afterward and Mom said she'd give me a hundred dollars for new clothes. Oh, I should check how much money I have for the haircut and any wardrobe extras.

I squirm into my closet, reach into the back corner, and pull out my bank. It feels heavy and my coins clink noisily inside it. There should be a nice stash because I've been saving my allowance for months. I take off the lid and shake out the pitcher's contents over my bedspread.

Holy moly. The coins are still there, but my paper money's gone. All of it. Every last bill.

I suddenly picture the bills Shay flashed at the thrift store. At the time, I didn't believe she was from the future, so I hardly questioned where she got the money. Now, with my bank emptied, she's a prime suspect.

But she wouldn't steal from me. She's a guest in my home. No one would stoop that low.

Then again, she ate half a box of Oreo cookies the very first day she got here. She took Mom's clothes. And she stole books from the school library.

Shay Saunders is a thief. She took my money.

And the whole time I've been stewing over her tonight, she's probably been getting drunk and making out with the one guy I hate most at school.

I pound my fist on the desk again.

Ow. Stupid idiot Tyler.

"**Bummer I didn't get** to meet your family tonight," Rick says over the blare of "Stairway to Heaven" on the car radio.

I laugh.

"I'm totally serious."

"Oh."

"How long have you lived at that house? What school were you at before?" he asks.

"Slow down," I say. I mean on the questioning, but also his driving. I still can't get over that cars don't have shoulder belts. Or airbags. Or antilock brakes. I could die. And it would totally suck to die in 1978, before I was even born.

"Sorry, babe." Rick eases up on the gas, which allows him to slide his hand up and down my leg as if he's playing the guitar solo on the radio.

"This song is so hot. You're so hot," I tell him.

"Right back at you, babe."

I've managed to stop his questions for now. But I can't help thinking I'm doing the same messed-up things in 1978 that I did in 2006.

When we get to John's house, only about twenty people are there. The girls are all pretty. Most of the guys are cute. The others must be athletic or funny. Led Zeppelin wails at the party too. It's playing on an album, a giant black disk that slowly spins around on a wooden box. The scratchy music blares through speakers the size of toddlers. Most of the kids are gathered around the keg on the back porch or the bong on the orange shag carpeting inside.

Rick and I drink beer on the couch, watch the group around the bong, and kiss. We talk to people. A guy gives us a thumbs-up. Rick licks my ear. The room crowds with kids. I sit halfway on Rick's lap because six people fill the couch. I play with his chest hairs and try to avoid his girly shell necklace. We drink more beer. My head gets foggy.

A guy with hair as long and pretty as mine turns on the TV. *Saturday Night Live* is on, with John Belushi and Gilda Radner running around in bee suits.

"This is life, right? I mean, live," I shout to Rick over the TV show/Village People song/girl next to me saying she feels sick. "Not a rerun. It's a classic. Or going to be one, anyway."

Rick takes his tongue out of my ear long enough to say, "Yeah, they're gnarly."

John Belushi is probably just getting hooked on drugs. I should call him right now at the TV studio and tell him to stop or he'll die. He wouldn't listen to me. Especially since I'm slurring my words.

Why was I sent back twenty-eight years? It's not like I'm doing any good here. I'm never going to warn people about stuff or save anyone from anything. I can barely help myself.

Maybe I'm supposed to find my mom. Tell her not to have

a kid because she'll be nothing but a screwup. That even when she's sent back in time, all she'll do is what she does in 2006—fool around with guys and get wasted. I'll tell Mom I'm not worth the monthly check from Texas.

"What are you crying for?" Rick says.

Damn. My tears are flowing as freely as the beer.

He puts my face against his hard chest and strokes my cheek.

I wonder if 1978 mascara is waterproof. *How shallow*, I tell myself, and cry some more. "I'm sorry," I tell Rick.

"Don't be sorry. It just freaks me out to see chicks cry. Especially you."

I guess Rick isn't The Dick that Tyler thinks he is.

"You're so sweet," he says. "I'm falling for you."

Maybe I really can be sweet in 1978. Maybe I'm falling for Rick too.

No. Sex is power. My mother's mantra. Mine too. *Boys are to be used, not to be loved.* And look what happened to the Great Gatsby. The dude was all in love and then he died. I think I heard that, anyway. I should finish reading it to be sure.

I also need to read those physics books and figure out how to get home. How did I even get here? How did I go from post-sex bliss to 1978 shock? *Think, Shay.*

Oh. My. Gawd. I wasn't just sitting in the tub before I was zapped to 1978.

Sex. I need to have sex. It's the missing ingredient. Rick is my ticket home. And not a bad way to get there. He's a hot guy and I can have sex without fear. There's no AIDS in 1978. Maybe not even herpes. We just need birth control.

I fling my arms around Rick's tank of a torso and whisper, "Let's get some champagne, take a bath, and get nasty."

He opens his mouth, but no words come out. Just a giant grin.

I press myself into him, against his bulging designer jeans. "Come on."

"Let's find a bedroom. Or my car," he says.

"No. Bath and champagne."

A minute later, he's begging his friend John for champagne.

"Get a condom too," I whisper. The thought of having a baby is awful enough, but having a baby in 1979 who would be older than me in 2006 is so creepy that I high-five his friend when he pulls a condom from his pocket and slips it into Rick's palm.

John finds a bottle of champagne in the fridge, just like Jake did a few days ago, a few decades in the future. Yes! I'm going home to 2006.

Rick opens the champagne with a loud pop. We pour it into our empty beer cups and stumble to the upstairs bathroom and lock the door.

I run the bath water and start taking off my clothes. Rick stands frozen as I step out of my dress and undo my grandma-bra. He sputters, "You sure you want to do this?" which I guess is pretty gentlemanly or whatever of him.

I nod. "Take your clothes off."

So Rick forces his eyes off my bod, puts the condom on the ledge of the bathtub, and gets naked fast. Unfortunately, he doesn't take off his puka shell necklace.

I kick aside our piles of clothes and reach my arms around his neck. He kisses me and rubs my back while I undo the clasp for those damn shells. I don't want my last image of 1978 to be of Rick's foofoo necklace.

We make out standing in the bathroom, then take a breather to climb into the tub. The warm water feels good.

"I don't want to do anything you don't want to do," Rick says.

"I want to go all the way," I whisper in his ear.

"It's my first time," he mumbles.

"You're kidding." I don't tell him it's, like, my fiftieth time. I don't ask if he's sure he's ready. I just get on top of him, pull the condom on him, and guide him in me.

He tells me I'm beautiful. He says he's falling in love.

I kiss him so he'll stop talking. He's just a body to have sex with, that's all, to get back, or forward anyway, to my own bedroom and my own friends, who never wear huge collars or talk about physics. *Sex is power,* I tell myself.

I close my eyes. Rick is moaning. The water is sloshing. I'm working hard. I feel a little sick from the beer, and a little guilty about Rick, and my mind's a lot on 2006. I wonder whether my old life is worth the trip.

It's all useless, anyway. The champagne, the sex, the bathtub, Rick. Even after I make Rick get out of the tub and I lie in it silently wishing myself home, I don't go anywhere. I'm still stuck in the 70's. And I can't help wishing my first time with Rick hadn't been in a bathroom at a party when we were both drunk.

The Dick and Shay are stumbling up the driveway. I open the door for her. The Dick stands beside her, grinning as if he just had the best night of his life.

She waves him off and staggers into the house, bleary-eyed, wet-haired, and shivering. She appears so soft and so hard at the same time. Her shoulders slump and her feet drag, yet her black eyes have fight in them. Heavyweight championship possibilities, even.

"How was the party?" I point to her wet hair. "Did you go swimming or something?"

She shakes her head and winds her way past me.

I follow her through the hallway, into the living room, and to the good sofa we're not supposed to use. She crumbles onto it.

I join her, sitting straight as a Boy Scout, with a foot of space between us.

"I tried to get home tonight," she says. "You know, my real house. I got in the bathtub with Rick, like I did with Jake the day I left."

"I don't want to hear about you and The Dick in the bathtub," I manage to sputter.

"It didn't work, anyway."

"You stole my money," I say.

She just sits there on the good couch, next to me but ignoring me, which gets me even madder.

"You got into my closet, all the way into the back of it, went through my stuff, and stole every cent I had in my bank."

She shrugs. "Not any of the cents. Juss, just the bills. I needed clothes. I'm sorry. It was only, like, forty-six dollars."

"That's a lot of money, actually."

"If I'm here for much longer, I'll find a way to pay you back."

"Maybe instead of spending your energy on The Dick, you should try to get a job."

"For your information, I have a . . ." She shakes her head. "What are you, my damn mother?"

"I bet she's worried sick."

"I bet you have no idea what you're talking about." Her voice is shaky. Not just drunk-shaky, but sad-shaky. "I'll pay you back."

"It's okay." I'm such a sap, I even smile at her. "I'm sure you needed the money."

She doesn't return the smile. "It's not okay."

"Look, I'll help you, Shay. If you want, I'll try to get you home. We need to research and do some real experiments, make guestimates, basically."

"Don't say *basically*. Another nerd word. Or guesti, guesti, guestiwhatever."

Then she closes her eyes and falls asleep on the good sofa.

I pick her up in my arms. She's warm, despite being passed out cold. I want to kiss her so badly, even though her breath smells like alcohol and she just fooled around with The Dick, and my entire body is killing me getting her up the stairs. Not to mention she'd probably slap me. But, man, I want to kiss her.

"I'll pay you back," she mumbles.

"No. It's all right."

I take her to Heather's room and set her on the trundle bed. As I walk back to my bedroom, I hug myself a little, trying to keep the sensation of holding her in my arms.

16

I sleep in late. When I finally get up, I take a long, hot shower and two aspirin. Then I throw on some clothes and go down to the kitchen. Heather's there, wearing a bright turquoise scarf around her neck. "You look pretty," I tell her, then can't help adding, "Told you so."

Heather's cheeks are flushed now. "It's just a scarf. I thought I'd give it a try."

"You thought right." I find a Tab and start chugging it.

Tyler walks in.

I spill my soda.

He looks hot. Besides his improved browline, he got the hairstyle I recommended, a side-parted layered cut, blow-dried for fullness.

"We're going shopping today, right?"

I nod.

"Awesome." He smiles at me. His lips seem fuller, his teeth whiter, his eyes deeper.

I spill more of my Tab.

The shock has worn off by the time we leave. Tyler doesn't look so hot when he's driving his mother's station wagon, a piece of crap with rust spots breaking through like chicken pox.

"In 2006, I never let myself be seen in a heap like this. This is a favor, not a date," I tell him.

"In 1978," he says, "you should appreciate whatever wheels you can get."

The Gap is our first stop at the mall. I pick out 501 jeans for him, a flannel shirt, and brown corduroy pants. The corduroy kills me, but I have to go with what's in now.

He points to a rack of polyester pants.

I shake my head. "Even I have my limits. I know polyester is in style now for some insane reason, but, like, gross. Let's get you some surfer clothes."

"But I don't surf."

"That's irreverent, Tyler. Or however you say that word."

"Irrelevant."

"Whatever. You don't need to surf to buy the clothes." I walk into Ocean Pacific, pull out a ruddy Hawaiian shirt, and put it up to Tyler.

He gives me the hang ten sign. "An excellent choice. You're a positive fountain of knowledge."

"Don't talk so fancy. Just say, like, 'you rock' or 'thanks.'"

"You're a rock. Thanks. To show my gratitude, let me use the coins you didn't steal from me to buy you lunch."

"Just say, 'Buy you lunch?'"

He points to me. "Lunch?"

"Much better. And, yeah, lunch would be great. But I can pay for myself, at least. I still have six dollars left from what I took from you."

Tyler rolls his eyes. "You're paying with my money."

"But you realize this is not a date, right?"

"You've said that twice today. I realize."

We go to an Italian place inside the mall. I get a side of spaghetti, salad, and a Tab. They don't have lite dressing. I don't know if it's been invented yet.

As we sit across from each other, twirling our pasta, making each other laugh, I'm not sure why this is not a date and why I didn't want it to be one. Tyler keeps putting his fingers through his hair, like he's not used to the new 'do. I'm tempted to smooth out his hair myself. *This is not a date,* I remind myself and look away.

At the next table, two of Rick's skinny blond-girl friends are sipping sodas. "Look to your left real fast, but don't stare," I tell Tyler. "Two popular girls from school are sitting right next to you."

He whips his head around and then back to me. "Wow. I hope they don't see me."

"Are you crazy? I thought you wanted to be popular."

"They call me and Evie 'Dip' and 'Drip.'"

"That was before your brow tweeze and haircut. I bet you were wearing dorky clothes then too."

He shrugs. "I guess."

"Ask them if they want to sit with us."

"Me?"

"No, your invisible friend next to you. Of course you."

"I . . . I can't."

"Listen. I didn't tweeze your eyebrows, research the perfect 1978 haircut for you, and spend the last hour and a half with you at the mall to hear you say you can't."

He sighs. "I guess I have to, huh?"

"Move it. Oh, wait. Hold on." I adjust his feathered hair around his face. Touching him does nothing for me. This is definitely not a date. "Okay, ask them."

Tyler clears his throat, then reaches over and taps the girl next to him on her bony shoulder. "I'd be honored if you charming ladies here—"

I kick his foot.

"I meant to say: Sit with us?"

The girl looks him over so long and so carefully, I half expect her to pull open his mouth to inspect his teeth. "Who are you?" she finally asks.

"Far-out," says her friend. "It's Tyler Gray. He looks totally different." She talks about him as if he's not, like, two feet away from her. "Did he get a haircut or something?"

"I like it," says the first girl.

"It's like Shaun Cassidy's hair without highlights," says the other girl. They both laugh at the same time and in the same way, little head bobs and quiet giggles with their lotioned, manicured hands over, but not touching their mouths. Just like my 2006 friends.

"Hey, Shay Saunders," the girl near me says. "Bitchin' dress."

"Thanks." It's Mrs. Gray's castoff, which I dyed in a huge pot of tea and shrank in the dryer.

"Let's sit with them," her friend says.

As they slide into our booth, they introduce themselves. They're Debbie M. and Debbie P. "We call ourselves the Double Ds," Debbie M says.

Double D my ass. More like a generous C. But Tyler's gaze goes right to her chest and dawdles there.

"You want to get some ice cream, Ty Ty?" Debbie M. tongues her upper lip almost as if she's flirting with him.

I've eaten at least 500 calories at lunch. "How about frozen yogurt instead?" I suggest.

The girls do their identical giggles again.

"Gross," Debbie M. says.

"Grody," Debbie P. says.

"What's the point of freezing yogurt?" Tyler asks.

"Good one, Ty Ty," Debbie M. says. She actually bats her eyelashes at him.

Gawd. "Well, I don't want ice cream."

"That's okay," Tyler says like I don't matter.

As soon as we get to Swensen's at the food court, Debbie M. says, "Ooh, wouldn't it be awesome to share a cone? We could each pick a flavor and get a triple scoop."

"I'll buy!" Tyler yelps before I even have time to roll my eyes.

He pays for the ice cream and holds it up like a trophy. "Who wants the first lick of my cone?"

I'm not sure whether his double tundra or whatever is on purpose.

Debbie M. grabs his ice cream cone, keeps it an inch from her mouth, sticks her tongue out, and slowly licks it.

"You should get paid for that," I mutter.

Tyler's mouth is open so wide, I'm tempted to smash the entire damn cone into it.

"Mom, I'm at a pay phone at Valley Mall," I tell her. "Can I please use your car a little longer than I'd asked for? Shopping is taking more time than expected." I don't tell her that I just made a movie date with three pretty girls and that I'm hoping to hold Shay's hand in the theater.

"Ty Ty." Debbie M. walks into the phone booth.

I back away to the rear wall of the booth, but she follows me.

"How much time, dear?" Mom asks.

"Uh . . ."

Debbie M. keeps pressing forward. She has a spot of ice cream on her nose. It's either wild cherry or chocolate. "Like what you see, Ty Ty?"

"Tyler, are you there?" Mom asks.

I step to the side. "Uh, I'll be home around five o'clock, okay?"

Debbie M. steps to the side too and moves in even closer to me.

"I suppose that's all right," Mom says.

"Great. Thanks." I hang up the phone.

"Shay said you two aren't on a date," Debbie M. says.

"You asked?"

"She told us. Twice." She holds two fingers up, then puts them on my chest.

Is Debbie M. actually coming on to me? She's standing so close now, I can tell it's wild cherry ice cream on her nose.

She leans her head into my chest, right above her fingers. "Did you hear me and Mike broke up last night at John's party?"

Holy smoke, I definitely think Debbie M. is coming on to me.

"We need to go if we want to see the movie." Shay walks toward us. Her arms are crossed and she's frowning. If I didn't know her better, I'd say she was jealous.

I make sure to sit next to Shay in the mall theater. I ignore the smell of popcorn around me so I can take in her warm cinnamon aroma. We share a box of Raisinets and our hands accidentally touch. It feels perfect. If I believed in that stuff, I'd call it karma.

As soon as the first preview airs, for *Rocky II,* Shay says, "They don't show ads?"

"Advertisements in movie theaters?" I ask. "That makes no sense. No one would pay two dollars for a ticket if they had to watch commercials first."

"You're right," Shay says. "A lot of people would stop going to theaters if they pulled crap like that."

"It also makes no sense that they're doing a sequel to *Rocky,"* I tell her. "The first one was good, but no one will watch another *Rocky* movie."

"You'd be surprised." She laughs. It's sexy.

I'm so close to taking her hand. I just need half an ounce more nerve.

When the preview for *Superman the Movie* comes

on, showing Superman carrying Lois Lane through the night sky, I get up a quarter ounce of nerve and whisper, "Maybe we can see that together."

She sniffs, not a haughty sniff, but one sounding like she's holding back tears.

I wonder if this is the time to take her hand. But I don't want it to seem like a mercy hold. "What's the matter?" I ask her.

"Superman. Christopher Reeve."

On the other side of me, Debbie P. says, "What a hunk," and Debbie M. says, "Love those tights," and both of them giggle again.

"You don't understand. The poor guy was in such good shape. I can't watch him." Shay gets up, passes me and the Double Ds, and walks up the aisle. The girls follow her.

I call Shay's name, but she's almost at the door, with the Double Ds right behind her. So I sit by myself through the previews, unsure what to do and what to make of everything going on. I lied to my mom again, Debbie M. seems to like me, and Shay is panicked about Superman.

Carpe diem, I tell myself. *Or, as Shay says, caveat emptor. Seize the day, buyer beware, you're going to hold Shay's hand.*

Grease has already started by the time the girls return. I don't hear Shay sniffling anymore, so maybe she's okay. She smells different now, lemony. Maybe it's from the bathroom soap.

Carpe diem, I tell myself. *Carpe her hand.*

I take a deep breath, then grab it.

Her hand seems colder and smaller and rougher than I imagined. But because I know it's Shay's, it feels great.

She squeezes my hand in return.

Shazam! This date, October 1, 1978, will go down in history as the best day of my life.

"Pass the Raisinets," Shay says.

She sounds far away.

Uh-oh. I look down at the hand I'm squeezing, follow it up to a skinny arm, a short neck, and then to the horsey face of Debbie M.

Yikes! The girls switched seats!

Debbie M. passes the Raisinets box to Shay. Then she puts her hand on my knee. Her hand travels to the inside of my thigh, on a slow, exploratory trip.

Exactly how many fingers does Debbie M. have? Enough to keep my leg very happy.

Just when I'm certain my left thigh will be in a permanent state of nirvana, she moves onto my right thigh. Then her hand roams my hips, my chest, and just about everywhere else that won't get us arrested. Though my gaze stays glued to the screen through the end of *Grease,* I have no idea what the movie is about. But I do enjoy the theatergoing experience.

When it's over, Debbie M. takes my hand again as we walk up the aisle. This time I don't resist. I can't resist. In fact, I can barely move.

"Let's go home," Shay snaps.

Debbie M. drops my hand, blows me a kiss, and calls out, "Bye-bye, Ty Ty."

"Later," Shay says as she rushes out of the theater.

Shay seems jealous, I held the wrong girl's hand, and my thighs are practically numb. What an awesome day.

17

"**Thanks for an awesome** day," Tyler gushes while he drives home.

"Yeah, whatever." I sneak a look at his face, intent on the road ahead, the face Debbie M. obviously thinks is all cute. "You know, I'm the one who changed your look," I blurt out.

"Should I call you Svengali?" he says.

"Seven Who?"

"Svengali," he says again.

"Yeah, whatever," I say again.

He laughs, almost as if I'm beneath him.

"Wow, you've changed," I tell him like it's not a compliment.

"Thanks." He obviously doesn't understand my tone of voice. He turns up the volume of the car radio and starts singing along. "Fever nights, fever nights fevuuuur." He bangs on the steering wheel in synch with the music. Or sort of in synch. "We have to go shopping again," he shouts over the radio. "I need a white disco suit just like Travolta's."

What have I done? Any improvement in his looks is outweighed by his new, crappy personality. "You want a disco suit?" I yell over the music. "Go buy it yourself."

He turns down the volume. "You don't have to be so rude."

"I'm through giving makeovers. I just want to chill."

"Chill? Are you hot?"

"Gawd." I reach over and turn off the radio. "*Chill* means *relax*. Which I plan to do as soon as I'm out of this damn station wagon."

But Heather meets me at the front door. "I need an outfit for my student council meeting tonight."

I shake my head. "I should stop messing with you guys. You were fine before."

"Please, Shay. I'm desperate."

She looks desperate. She's wearing a gray nylon dress with red heart buttons down the front. Total fashion catastrophe. So much for my chill plan.

I walk upstairs with her, search through her closet, and try not to groan. Her wardrobe looks like something worn only by Amish girl lumberjacks. I manage to find potential in a bright floral skirt. I use scissors and duct tape to make it thigh length while Heather sits on her bed with her hand over her mouth. If she gasps, I'm out of here.

She keeps her hand on her mouth, walks to the closet, and trots out a plain, scoop-collared, beige cotton blouse which could be part of a Girl Scout uniform. "I usually wear this with the skirt."

"Don't. Let's think outside the box."

She looks around. "What box?"

"Never mind. Have you outgrown any sweaters lately?"

She shows me a pile of clothes for Goodwill on the top shelf of her closet. It's not exactly a gold mine. More like an aluminum mine, if there are such things as aluminum mines. Whatever.

Aha. I pick out a tight white sweater which plunges in the back. I snip off the tag and tell Heather to wear the sweater backward. I pair the look with Heather's high-top sneakers, formerly wasted on basketball. I'm a fashion savant.

She models the new outfit for me, twirling in her skirt.

I pronounce her, "Cute, funky, and a little indecent."

"Is that good?"

"It's great. And for the grand finale, let's bring on the makeup."

She stops twirling. "I don't wear makeup."

"Well, you should. Looking good is empowering. Boys will beg to do things for you. They'll be listening to your every beautiful word."

The power of face paint always thrills me. I make her eyes look darker and deeper, her nose cuter and smaller, her cheeks soft and pink. Coupled with the clothes make-over, Heather has gone from plain to pretty in a little over an hour.

"Heather, your ride is here," Mrs. Gray calls out. "Shay, can you help me with dinner?"

"Sure thing," I yell as we walk out of the bedroom.

Tyler's in the hallway. He points to Heather. "What did you do to her?"

"I brought out her beauty," I reply.

"Heather, you were already beautiful," he says.

"I know she was. I just played up what's already there."

Heather smiles. "I think I look bitchin'."

"You're not supposed to look bitchin'. You're only fifteen." He shakes his head. "Jeez, Shay."

"It's okay to make you over, but not your sister? Please," I say.

"I like looking bitchin'," Heather says. "Let's go."

I follow her downstairs. She heads for the front door and I rush to the kitchen.

I won't let worries about my sister ruin one of the best days of my life. I can't wait to tell Evie what happened. "Hey!" I shout into the mouthpiece as soon as she says hello. "You wouldn't believe who I hung out with at Valley Mall today!"

"Shay?"

"Yeah, Shay. But also two of the Debbies. Debbie M. and Debbie P. Not Debby with a y. You should have seen the way Debbie M. licked my ice cream."

"So sorry I missed that." She doesn't seem sorry at all.

"I actually spent half the day with three popular girls."

"*Actually* is a nerd word, remember?"

"That's right. I hope I didn't say it in front of the Double Ds. Evie, it was like *Debbie Does Dallas* here. Debbies Do the Mall." I'm talking so fast, I'm practically panting. "After we finished our ice cream, we saw *Grease* at the mall theater."

"We talked about that movie last weekend. We both

thought it sounded dumb, remember?" She sounds much less enthused than I expected she'd be.

"Who cares about the quality of the movie, Evie? Think about me sitting with three of the most popular girls at school."

"They just wanted to drool over John Travolta. He's a flash in the pan. I didn't even like him in *Welcome Back, Kotter*."

I shake my head. "Can't you be happy for me?"

"Those girls called us Dip and Drip to our faces, remember?"

"Well, I phoned to tell you about it. So, see you at school tomorrow." I hang up.

Ick. Mrs. Gray is wearing that pink polyester dress again.

Today she's accessorized with bright pink eye shadow, pink rouge, Day-Glo pink lipstick, and a pink gingham apron. I guess it's better than my mom's plunging necklines and tight jeans. I'd rather have a mother who heads the Fashion Don't list than one with a lifetime membership as a MILF.

But Mrs. Gray is not your mother, I remind myself. *You're just here until Tyler and Evie figure out how to get you home.* I sigh.

"Are you okay, dear?" Mrs. Gray asks.

"Yes, fine. What are we fixing for dinner tonight?"

"First, I want to give you something." She holds up a pink gingham apron which matches hers. "I sewed this for you."

I open my mouth but no words come out.

"You're a sweet girl, Shay." She hands me the apron.

No one ever sewed anything for me before. In fact, my mom's given me most of my presents in cash.

"Is it okay?" Mrs. Gray asks me.

I can't talk.

"Try it on, dear."

I want to, but my hands fumble too much. Mrs. Gray puts the bib of the apron over my head, then ties the pink bow at my back. I use the bottom of the apron to wipe my eye.

"It's perfect for you."

Me? A pink gingham apron perfect for me? Well, why the hell not?

"I can teach you to sew more of these if you'd like."

I nod. There's nothing I'd like better.

18

I awake with a start late at night. Someone is arguing. "It's about time you got here!" Mom yells.

Holy cow! Something horrible must be happening because Mom never raises her voice. I get out of bed, put on my bathrobe, and start to creep down the stairs.

Dad is yelling back. I stop halfway down the stairs and sit on the landing.

"You're never home," Mom says.

"I work hard for this family." Dad stands by the front door, still in his overcoat.

Mom faces him with her hands on her hips. "What if I want to work?"

He has to clutch the doorknob and take deep breaths.

I have to clutch my knees and take deep breaths.

Finally, Dad says, "Why would you want to work? You've either been getting your consciousness raised or watching those Marlo Thomas specials."

"I could have my own TV show. I could start a magazine."

"Good Lord!"

"I can find things to do besides wait for you!" she yells.

"I can too." He walks out the front door and slams it shut.

I race downstairs. Mom is still standing in the hall-way.

"Mom! Run outside before Dad leaves. Ask him to come back."

"Maybe I don't want him back." Her voice is too calm.

"Of course you do, Mom. He's your husband. He's my father. We're supposed to be a family."

"What about me?" she asks.

"You're Dad's wife."

"I'm more than that." She says it like there's something wrong with being a wife. "Shay—"

"Oh, no, Mom. Not Shay again. Don't listen to Shay."

Dad's car starts in the driveway. "Hurry, Mom. You can still catch him," I tell her.

She pushes past me. Instead of going outside to save her marriage, she walks upstairs.

"Mom!"

Dad's car pulls away.

I'm awoken by squeaks and lurches and sighs.

It's Heather rummaging through her closet and throwing clothes on the floor.

The clock on her nightstand shows 6:17. Way too early, especially because there's no coffee in this house.

Heather catches me with one of my eyes half open. "You're up! Thank you for helping me last night!"

I yawn. "So I take it the meeting went well?"

"That's a total understatement. I was compared to both Jaclyn Smith and Kate Jackson!"

"Awesome. Who?"

"You know. *Charlie's Angels.* The brunettes. And Roger Hyashita, who's not only a senior but student council president, said I looked bitchin'. Me! Bitchin'!" She bounces on my bed. "Can you believe it?"

"I definitely believe it." What the hell does *bitchin'* mean anyway? Something good I guess. "You go, girl."

"Huh? Go where?"

"I mean, that's great."

"And it's all thanks to you," Heather says.

"Not all of it." Ninety-nine percent of it. "It's your bitchin' face and body too."

Though I'm half asleep, I suddenly realize I'm making a difference. Maybe that's why I was sent here. Maybe as soon as I've changed enough people's lives, whoever or whatever sent me to 1978 will bring me home. I think I saw that plot last year on a Christmas TV movie.

Heather's bouncing again. "So can you please, please, please help me with another outfit today?"

I rub my eyes, haul myself out of bed, dig through the closet, and hand her a turtleneck sweater.

"That? I wore that for the last choral performance."

"We'll cut off the turtleneck part. Here." I toss a navy jumper to her.

"My mom bought that jumper for me. It looks like a school uniform." she says.

"Never question my fashion sense. Put it on. Backward."

When she wears the jumper backward, it looks funky and totally plays up her boobs. "You're the best," Heather says.

"I know. This morning, wear the outfit just like your mother intended. On the way to the bus stop, we'll tape up the jumper to thigh level, turn it around, cut up your sweater, and get everything looking, um, bitchin'."

"Cool. And can you do my makeup again? I'm allowed to use it. I just never did before you came."

"Sure." I give her full-on, long-lashed, charcoal-eyed, red-lipped face paint. She looks hot. I teach her how to throw her shoulders back to show off her chest.

After a few minutes of practice, we head downstairs.

Tyler's in the kitchen, shoveling bright bits of *Hardy Boys* cereal into his mouth.

I start chugging a Tab.

"Where's Mom?" Heather asks.

Tyler furls his improved brows. "Still sleeping."

"Really?" Heather says it like she just found out the guy who played Mike Brady is gay. Doesn't Mrs. Gray ever get to sleep in?

"Mom was up late last night. Fighting with Dad over Shay's brilliant plan for her to get a job." Tyler stands up and pushes out his chair. "Shay, we need to work on that time travel project. Instead of meddling with my parents, you should try to help yourself." He grabs his backpack, heads out the front door, and slams it behind him.

19

Five minutes after AP Physics starts, Mr. Spitz stops his gravitational pull lecture mid-sentence and stares at the door. As does the rest of the class.

Shay walks into the room and stands by the doorway. She's one of the few girls here without black-framed glasses, greasy hair, pimples, or some combination thereof.

After a long silence, Mr. Spitz finally sputters, "Can I help you?"

"I'm fine," she says. While the class gapes silently, Shay seats herself on the left side of the room, crosses her ankles, and folds her hands on top of the desk. She actually looks sweet.

Mr. Spitz opens his mouth, leaves it hanging for approximately thirty seconds, and then clamps it shut. He wanders to his desk and checks his notes. Finally, he says, "Why are you here, Miss . . . ?"

"Saunders. Shay Saunders. I'm Tyler Gray's friend, just visiting. I'm going to audit your class," she says to Mr. Spitz. Says, not asks.

"What about your own classes?" he sputters.

"Oh, I'm a dropout. I heard you were so inspirational, your class was just the thing to get me to re-enroll in school again."

What can he say? Apparently, nothing. He stands in frozen silence for another minute before nodding, clearing his throat, and teaching again.

Mr. Spitz actually can be inspirational. He uses rubber bands, magnets, and metal balls to illustrate gravity in space. It's fascinating.

At the end of class, Shay walks to my desk and stands over me. My eyes are directly across from her very tight red sweater, which probably matches the color of my face. "Welcome to your first class," I manage to say. "What did you think of it?"

She shrugs. "It was cool how the teacher explained physics with rubber bands and stuff."

"You just used *physics* and *cool* in the same sentence."

"Gawd, I guess I did."

"I hope my dad comes back," I say.

"Assuming your mom will take him back."

"Did you say something else to her?"

"No, Tyler. Give it a rest. Not everything is my fault, you know."

She has a point. Dad was pulling late nights for a long time before Shay ever got here. And I know it bothers Mom. Last night was just the first time I heard her yell at Dad instead of crying in her bedroom. "Shay." I look her in the eyes instead of in the sweater. "I'm sorry about this morning when I acted so . . ."

"Sulky? Pissy? Juvenile?"

"I was thinking more along the lines of *sensitive.*"

She rolls her eyes. "Whatever. Let's chill. You want to walk over to the lunch area together? We're eating with Rick and the Debbies today, right?"

"We are? All right!" I stuff my backpack as fast as possible. "I'll meet you there. First, I want to ask Evie to join us."

After buying a turkey sandwich, I set my tray on the table and sit across from Evie. "Hey, you missed a good movie Sunday," I say. "You like my haircut?"

She glances at me, says, "Nice," then returns to her horsemeat surprise, which the cafeteria calls beef stew.

"Shay picked out a bunch of trendy clothes for me too."

"Just call her Svengali."

"I did. She didn't understand. She does like to change people, huh?"

Evie keeps eating.

"If we had a dog, Shay would probably cut its fur, dye it pink, and enter it in kennel shows. If she found a mouse, she'd give it assertiveness training."

Evie smiles at that. "I just hope she doesn't dump you as soon as we help her with that time travel project."

"Even if we wanted to help, we couldn't," I say. "Because if time travel is even possible, don't you think scientists would have figured it out by now? And since they couldn't, why in the world would high school seniors be able to? Even a genius like you."

"Imagination is more important than knowledge. You told me that."

"That's actually a quote from Einstein," I whisper. "He's uncool."

"Who cares?"

"I do, Evie. Shay's helping me become popular. She and the Debbies even invited me to their lunch table."

"You're not actually going to sit with them, are you?"

"Of course I am. You too. Let's boogie."

"*Boogie*? Where the heck is my old friend Tyler?"

"What's wrong with instantly upgrading our standing at school?" I point to the popular table. Shay is squeezed tight against The Dick, groping his bicep.

"That looks like a downgrade to me."

I stand and pick up my tray. "You coming with me or not?"

"Not. And where's the money you promised me for lying to your mother?"

"Shay stole it." I leave the table.

As I approach Debbie M., she shouts, "Ty Ty! You made it! Alone! When I saw you in the nerd area, I freaked out that you were going to bring one back with you." She shivers.

I feel like shivering myself.

"Sit here!" She points to approximately three inches of space next to her.

"I can't fit there. Hey, I see a spot next to Shay."

"Silly Ty Ty. I'll sit on your lap."

"But how am I supposed to eat, Debbie M.?"

She stands up. Her blouse is so sheer it's practically invisible. "Call me Deb Deb."

"Okeydokey, Deb Deb." If she asked me to now, I'd call her Supreme Goddess of the Universe.

I sit on the bench, and she climbs onto my lap and leans against my chest. I think, *Who needs to eat, anyway?*

But I can't help looking down the bench—past the Weeble who tripped Evie in the hallway last week, past Loose Lori and Spacy Stacy, past Shay as she gets on The Dick's lap—and peering toward my old lunch table. It's too far away to see Evie. I hope she's not eating alone.

Debbie M. twists her head toward me and kisses my cheek. She smells like a grove of rotting lemons. "So Shay says you're throwing a gnarly party."

"Definitely. For her birthday. We're having a kegger."

"My birthday girl." The Dick grabs Shay's face and kisses her.

Debbie M. grabs my face. She puts her lips close to mine.

"Deb Deb," I whisper to stall for time.

"Ty Ty."

"Deb Deb."

I remove her hands from my face and check my watch. Phew. Only approximately two more minutes until the lunch bell rings. "Deb Deb, would you mind getting off my lap so I can eat some lunch?"

20

The past week has been pretty cool. I've got a little routine going—riding the bus to school, reading books backstage in the theater, going to physics class, eating lunch in the cafeteria, working at the diner, taking the bus home, and hanging with the Grays.

It's not a bad life. I even like physics. And I'm getting into reading, secretly, of course. I returned those beauty books to the library and swiped *Othello* and *Valley of the Dolls*. Shakespeare is almost as steamy as Jacqueline Susann.

Lunchtime is great today. Tyler's sitting with us, everyone seems jazzed about my birthday party, and John says his brother can get us a keg.

Then Rick starts in on me again. "Will you let me walk you to fourth period today, or are you going to split again?"

I give him a dumb-girl shrug. He can't walk me to class after lunch because I don't go to class after lunch. And I can't tell him that, no matter how many times he asks. He always wants to know stuff about me. *Who do you have for English? Where's your locker? How come I didn't see you at the assembly yesterday?* I keep trying to distract him with my hands and mouth, but I don't know how much longer I can keep up the Sexy Mystery Woman thing.

I wish I had my cell. When you eat lunch or walk down the school hallways without a cell phone against your ear or an iPod, you actually have to talk to people. It's weird. So even though the school is an open campus, people keep asking where I'm going. Rick especially.

"If you'd let me walk you to class, I could carry that for you." He points to my feet, at the linen tote bag Mrs. Gray made me.

If Rick looked inside and saw my work apron, which I just washed but is still disgusting, and my books, he'd probably ask a million more questions. So I clamp my feet around the bag, put my hands on Rick's open shirt, and play with the hairs on his chest.

He grabs my hands. "Come on, Shay. Answer me for once. Why can't I walk you to your next class? Are you embarrassed to be seen with me?"

The bell rings. "Let go of me, Rick," I say.

He does. "Sorry. I just want to be with you, that's all."

"We don't need to walk around the halls, like, all arm-in-arm cutesy."

"We don't need to, but I want to. Don't you?" he asks.

"It's not just about *wants*, Rick." What I really want is to walk to Krasno's Diner as fast as possible before anyone sees me and before I'm late to work. I get up, smile at him, say, "Catch you later," and rush off.

He follows me.

I walk toward the school entrance. Once he sees I'm leaving, I'm sure he'll turn around and head to his next class.

I go off campus. He keeps following me. I spin around and ask, "What the hell are you doing?"

"Let me take your bag for you," he pleads.

I shake my head. "If you must know, I'm going to my part-time job, okay?"

"That's cool, Shay."

"No, Rick, it's not cool. It's at a decrepit old diner. I spend fifteen hours a week there cleaning crap off stuff."

He shrugs. "You want company?"

"Rick. You don't understand. I put my hair in a pony, wear an old apron, and end up greasy and smelly. It's not sexy. Trust me, you don't want to see me in that dive scrubbing dishes."

"Man. Here I am, totally stoked you're being honest with me for once, and you act like all I care about is your looks."

"But . . ."

"As long as I'm missing fourth period to walk my girlfriend to her job, I might as well help her a little."

"Girlfriend?" I gulp.

"For sure." He takes the tote bag from me. "Whoa, that apron really is ugly." He laughs. "I bet you look cute in it. What else you got in the bag?"

"None of your—"

He peers in. "It's books, right? You like to read?"

"Well, I—"

"I can't believe how lucky I am. Finding a hardworking girl who's foxy and smart too."

"And what about sweet?" I'm pushing it now.

"Sweet to the max."

We hold hands all the way to Krasno's Diner. Then Rick sits in a booth drinking a soda while I scrub the tables in my awful diner getup. After I've cleaned every table I can and have to head to the kitchen, I stop at his booth and tell him good-bye.

He kisses me, even though I'm sweaty and the ponytail is a bad look for me and my apron is already dirty. And for the first time ever, I get lost in a kiss.

It's especially hard to leave Rick when I'm faced with stacks of dirty muffin pans, metal bowls sticky with dried pancake batter, and smelly breakfast dishes. At least Mariel's in the kitchen. We stand side by side at the two sinks. Who would have thought I'd be in an old apron, scrubbing stuff, next to my former housekeeper? Or, like, future housekeeper.

I close my eyes, try to breathe through my mouth, and imagine the shoes I'll buy with my pay—a pair of stilettos, kick-ass boots I bet Rick would love, high-top sneakers like Heather's.

"You are good day?" Mariel's English is as atrocious as ever.

I open my eyes. *"Háblame en español."* Talk to me in Spanish.

"¿Cómo sabe usted español?" Meaning, roughly, *How the hell does a dumb white chick like you know Spanish?*

Working in a greasy spoon for minimum wage, I'm not about to say I picked up Spanish from the housekeepers I've had all my life. Instead, I shrug and ask, "Do you recognize me?"

"¿Qué es recognize?"

I translate it for her.

"*No le reconozco.*"

Damn. She has no idea who I am.

"You help me *inglés*?"

I shrug. Why not? I've been helping everyone else around here. And if I can get Mariel to speak halfway decent English, it might even make things easier for me in 2006, on the off chance I ever return to 2006. "You sure you don't know who I am?" I ask her in Spanish.

"Are Shay. Are worker here."

"Okay, first lesson. Say, '*You* are Shay. *You* are *a* worker here.'"

"*You* are Shay. *You* are *a* worker here. *¿Bien?*"

"*Bien.*" Whoever knew I could tutor anyone? "Mariel, do you think someone who hasn't gotten an A since sixth grade could actually be smart? Can you *become* smarter somehow? Like, by reading, or talking to geniuses, or taking physics classes and crap like that?"

"Slow, *por favor,*" she says.

"If a guy says you're smart, it's probably a line so he can get into your pants, right?"

"*No comprendo.*"

I talk slowly. "Two boys told me I am smart. They are probably lying, right? Boys want girls to like them, so they lie."

"No, no, no all. Some yes, but no all. One or two boys maybe no lie." She giggles.

It's good to hear that high-pitched laugh of hers again. We used to watch *Jerry Springer* together sometimes. Even though I doubt she understood what people were shouting about, the show was always good for laughs.

"Maybe boys think are smart," she says. *"Todavía le respetan."*

"No. Guys don't respect me." I scrub the muffin pan so hard, it shines.

"No all boys same." Mariel stops washing dishes. She stares up at me with her warm brown eyes.

"Rick Bowden might be different. I'm pretty sure he likes me for more than my looks. I mean, really likes me." I put the muffin pan on the rack to dry, then spray the sink faucet until all the crap goes down the drain. "Tyler Gray might be different. We slept in his bedroom together and he didn't even make one move on me."

"¿Qué dice?"

"He carried me up to my room when I was passed out drunk and he didn't even try anything then. Some boys are good. Right, Mariel?"

"Some boys are good."

I wipe my hands on my apron. "A girl who works hard and acts smart and sweet and helpful can get respect. Some guys really appreciate that."

I *thought things* were okay with Shay, but I was wrong. I get home from school to find Mom made over, or Shayed-over. For one thing, Mom doesn't have an apron on. Worse, she's wearing teenager clothes: a bright yel-

low T-shirt and stiff, tight jeans that say "Gloria Vander-
bilt" on the back pocket. Last week, Dad came back after
their fight; but tonight, when he sees Mom in her getup,
he might leave for good.

I walk upstairs without even stopping for a snack. It's
slow going with my backpack weighing me down. I picture Evie stooped under her huge green backpack loaded
with books. Sometimes we studied together at lunch.
More often we played backgammon with the travel set
she carted around. I wonder if she even brings it to school
anymore. Maybe she's playing with somebody else.

By the time I make it into my bedroom and set down
my backpack, the inside of my chest feels raw. I sit on
my bed and stare at Albert Einstein. "How could a person be popular and lonely at the same time?" I ask him.
"Should I apologize to Evie? How do I keep my parents
together? Was Shay sent here to screw up my life or make
it better?"

Always keep questioning, Albert used to say. I go to my
desk, open my physics book, search the index for tidal
waves, and get to work.

I hole up in my room until it's time for dinner, which
smells like the school chemistry lab.

"What is this?" Dad points to the stench-emitting glass
bowl of lumpy brown substance.

"Hamburger Helper. It's new." Mom, sitting down for a
change, passes the bowl to him.

"Where's our real dinner?" He slides it back to her.

The movement of the bowl spreads the stink across the table. I resist the urge to plug my nose.

"If you don't like it, make something else," she says.

My leg starts shaking, but I manage to take the Hamburger Helpless, dole out two spoonfuls, and pass the bowl to Heather.

"It smells good, Mom," Heather says with a straight face.

I pick at the meat. It tastes like salted, burned dog food. Not that I've ever eaten salted, burned dog food. Or even plain dog food.

"What in heaven's name have you been doing all day, Marlene?" Dad says. "Obviously not cooking."

"For one thing, I've been filling out a job application," Mom says. "I'm going back to work."

I gag on the meat crumbs.

Dad shakes his head. "What has gotten into you?"

"I need to find myself," Mom says.

"Find yourself? Find yourself?" Dad's sputtering like a Chevy Vega. "You're right here. In this beautiful seventy-two-thousand-dollar house where you belong. You find yourself, and I lose a wife and the kids lose a mother."

"I found the perfect job, if they'll take me. It'll still let me be home before the kids. Shay told me about it."

Shay, Shay, Shay. I knew it. She probably recommended the Hamburger Helpless too.

"I'm going to be the lunch lady at the high school cafeteria."

21

Ugh. Mom is (1) at my school, (2) serving kids lunch, (3) in a hairnet. But besides the hairnet and the overwhelming odor of overcooked canned peas, there's something different about her today. I can't figure out what it is exactly.

Evie stands in front of me in the cafeteria line, staring at Mom. We haven't spoken since our argument that day in the lunch area. She's not wearing her Godzilla-sized backpack. Someone at the lunch tables must be watching it for her. I wonder who.

"Evie! It's lovely to see you," Mom says.

"You're working at the . . ." She adjusts her glasses. The genius seems confused.

"I'm officially a lunch lady!" She says *lunch lady* like it's a good thing. "Tyler didn't tell you about my new job?"

I look away.

"You haven't been over in a while, Evie," Mom says. "You kids aren't having a tiff, are you?"

"Actually, we—" Evie starts to say.

I interrupt. "Actually, we're fine."

"Move it," a chubby girl behind me mutters.

Mom gives Evie a square hamburger and burnt fries. "I'd like you to eat vegetables too, dear."

She nods, a genius left speechless, and staggers off.

I step forward and point to the burgers and fries.

As Mom hands me my food, she says, "You and Evie seem so unhappy. Tyler, dear, you know I hate when you make that sad-sack face."

The chubby girl behind me giggles.

"What if your face froze with that frown on it?" Mom asks.

The chubby girl says, "Yeah, don't be a sad sack, Tyler, dear."

I stomp off, but can't help stopping and staring at Mom one more time. It finally dawns on me what's different about her today. She's smiling.

I head toward my new friends, or, if not exactly friends, friendly acquaintances. But first I take a detour to find Evie. She's sitting with some guys from the math club who I hardly ever talk to anymore. They're laughing. It's not that fake laughter like with the popular kids. I stand a few yards away, wondering what's so darn funny and why Evie's so darn happy without me.

Robert Beed, who most everyone else calls The Enquirer, taps me on the shoulder. "Are you okay?" he asks.

I peel my gaze away from Evie. "I'm fine."

"What's the scoop? Your parents get divorced?"

"No. Of course not. Why do you ask?"

"I saw your mom doling out food in the cafeteria."

So that's what this is. Another wonderful benefit of

Mom working at my school. "She wants to, okay? It's a feminist thing."

"Not so loud." The lunch monitor approaches with his fingers on his lips.

As Robert slinks off, the lunch monitor whispers, "Is everything all right with your family, Tyler? Business is booming at my uncle's typewriter store. I could put in a good word for your father if he needs a job."

I shake my head. "My family is just fine."

He puts his hand on my shoulder. "I see your mother's working in the cafeteria today."

"We're fine! My dad's fine. My mom's fine. Everyone's frickin' fine!"

"Shh!"

I rush to my lunch table.

Before I can get there, Janie Jensen grabs my arm. "I heard about your family. I am so, so sorry." She dabs at her eye. "I hope your father gets back on his feet soon. I noticed your sister's clothes are really tight on her now. I have some extra blouses she could use."

Argh!

I'm scrubbing the world's nastiest, oiliest, most ginormous pan. Mariel is next to me filling the dishwasher and practicing her English.

"Hey, Mariel, you want to go shopping with me? I need shoes."

"Use pay for shoes?"

"Say it this way, Mariel. 'Are you going to use your earnings to buy shoes?'"

"You family no need the money?"

"My family?" The Grays, I guess. "Uh, I owe them money."

"You live in they house." Mariel wipes around the sink.

"And they bought me clothes and pay for my food and keep me in Tab. The Grays take care of me." I feel my damn eyes tearing, and I can't even wipe them because my hands are coated with sausage grease.

Mariel dabs my tears with her fingers, which is, like, the nicest thing anyone's done for me—except for everything the Grays have done.

"Mariel." My voice wobbles.

"Is okay."

"No, it's not. The Grays are the best thing that ever happened to me." My voice is all quiet and quaky, but I don't stop. "Listen to me, Mariel. In the future you should never ignore your kid, or tell her she ruined your life, or buy stock in a company called Enron. You probably won't do any of these things, but some people do. And don't ever get a dragonfly tattoo if the artist sucks and it's right on your wrist where everyone can see it." The twin waterfalls come, and I sink my face into Mariel's shoulder so she can hold me in her doughy arms. "If I don't get back, will you water my fern?" I whisper. "It's about all I miss from home. The stupid fern. And you, I guess, too."

She doesn't say anything.

I step back so I can see her kind eyes. "You know what I'm talking about?"

"All be okay."

"But do you know, Mariel? Did you . . . Did you do something that day at Jake's house?"

"Who is Jake? Know what?"

"I guess not." I wipe my eyes with my arm. "Jake is nobody. Nobody important, anyway. I don't need shoes that bad. I mean, that badly." I better use correct English if I'm going to teach it.

Mariel smiles. "You shoes do fine."

She has a lovely smile. "You should go to school," I tell her. "You don't want to spend the rest of your life as a dishwasher or, like, a housekeeper, cleaning up after bratty, rich teenagers. Trust me on this."

"Maybe I go the school."

"Actually, learning can be fun. Don't tell anyone I said that."

Dinner is bright orange chemicals, also known as Kraft Macaroni and Cheese. I eat very little of it.

Dad pushes his plate toward the center of the table. He glares at Mom, sitting next to him. "I want my wife back, the one who cooks dinner—real dinner—and irons and starches my shirts." It's more of a command than a plea. My dad doesn't plead.

"The kids at school think we're having money trouble now," I say. "People offered me their old clothes today."

"For God's sake. That's it." Dad pounds his fist on the table. "You have to quit that job."

"I just started," Mom says.

"It's either the job or me."

Oh, no. "Dad, you're kidding, right?"

He shakes his head and picks up the *L.A. Times*.

Mom stares at him for a long time. Actually, she stares at the newspaper in front of his face for a long time.

This is when Mom decides what's important, I tell myself. *This is when she realizes we're the best part of her life, and stops listening to Shay's crazy ideas. This is when she digs out her recipes for Oriental chicken and red velvet cake.*

She clears her throat. "I choose the job."

22

Heather and I cleaned up from dinner an hour ago and Tyler went upstairs way before that, but Mrs. Gray is still at the dining room table. She's sitting alone with her hands clasped in front of her, gazing down. I stand at the opposite side of the table.

She doesn't look up.

"Um, Mrs. Gray?"

"Hmm?"

"Thank you for buying me clothes last month."

She keeps staring down.

I put three twenties in front of her on the table, which is a ton of money in 1978, especially when you're getting paid $2.30 an hour.

"Hmm?" she repeats.

I back away slowly and head upstairs.

On the way to Heather's room, I bump into Tyler. His eyes are narrowed, his jaw clenched tight. "I'm sorry. I never meant for your dad to leave," I tell him.

"Well, what did you think would happen?" He talks through gritted teeth. "I told you not to interfere."

"I just paid back your mom for the clothes she bought me. Next I'm going to return your forty-six dollars."

"Where did you get the money for my mom, anyway?"

Like I'm going to cop to washing dishes at a dive restaurant? Especially after Tyler said I was smart. *Dishwasher* is not the job for a smart girl. "It's not really your business where the money came from."

"Did The Dick give it to you? For recent services?"

I slap him across the face.

I'm standing in front of Shay and Heather's room. It's approximately 1:47 A.M., but I can't sleep. And it's not just because my left cheek is red and raw. I tap on the bedroom door and creak it open.

Heather is snoring softly, but Shay is sitting in bed with her arms crossed against her body.

"Meet me in the kitchen," I tell her before leaving the room.

I go downstairs and sit at the table, surrounded by my physics books and notebook and graphs, thinking that this might be the hardest thing I've ever had to do. And also thinking that my face hurts.

But I haven't spent all this effort perfecting my time travel theory for nothing. I have to send Shay back in order to save my family and my friendship with Evie, even if they don't realize they need saving. I'm like one of those religious crusaders, except I'm definitely right about who needs to be saved.

She arrives rubbing her eyes, looking deceptively innocent in one of Heather's flannel nightgowns, which I can't help noticing is snug around her chest. "What's the matter?" she asks.

"I've been studying physics books. I'm pretty sure I can get you home."

"Home?"

"To 2006."

Her dark eyes dart around like caught criminals.

"Don't you want to return to your family?"

She shrugs.

"And all your cool friends, and your boyfriend Jake?"

"He was never my boyfriend."

"If you leave now, I won't even mention the forty-six dollars you took from me." I open my notebook and start talking fast. "You see, if that guy Jake's bathtub was a perfect spherical shell, under Einstein's theory of gravity and Newton's postulates, it would exert no gravitational effects inside of it. If tidal forces hit the bathtub and hurled you back in time, you wouldn't feel the motion of travel even as it approached the speed of light."

She chews on her lip.

I stare down at my notes. "So, the tidal forces. I believe they're reversible. A bathroom fan over the water could have caused a whirlwind, mimicking the tides of travel. We need to place a fan over our bathtub, with you in it, of course, and speed it up and reverse it to send you home."

I wait for her to thank me. But she sits silently at the table.

I clear my throat. "You're the one who gave me the

idea of duct-taping a fan to the bathroom ceiling, instead of trying to wire it."

She doesn't respond.

"Because you've been cutting and duct-taping half of Heather's clothes."

Silence.

"Shay?"

"I like it here," she says, finally. "And other people—Heather, your mom, this girl Mariel—they appreciate me. I'm accomplishing things."

"Who's Mariel? Never mind. I don't care. Because you're not accomplishing anything." I touch my sore cheek for courage to continue. "Under the principle of self-consistency, time travelers don't change the past because they were always part of it. In other words, you can't do a darn thing here except cause temporary chaos."

"That's one theory," she says as if she knows anything about scientific theories. She's chewing her lip so hard, there's a drop of blood on it. "And to think I once believed you were—"

"I was what? A nerd? A geek? A dweeb? Maybe I was. But I'm not anymore."

"Kind. That's what I was going to say."

Oh. I touch my cheek again. "You have to leave, Shay."

"What about my birthday party?"

"Yes, Shay, exactly. If you leave now, you can celebrate with your real friends and family."

"They're all here." She stands up, pushes in her chair, and walks off.

I sit next to Evie on the bus this morning. She's slumped against the window, wearing a beige T-shirt and baggy jeans and cheap sneakers.

I used to look like that. Today I'm in an Ocean Pacific striped shirt and corduroy Levi's and Nikes. My big brown comb is in my back pocket, making me very trendy and making sitting uncomfortable. I grit my teeth, lift my head, and jut out my chin. According to Shay, a smug smirk and good posture are key components of cool.

"You okay?" Evie asks. "You hurt your neck?"

"I'm fine." I stare past her, out the window, at the billboard of Bo Derek in *10*. I wonder what Evie would look like with cornrowed hair. *Focus, Tyler.* "You should sit with me at lunch," I tell her.

"At the popular table? You don't need me there. You have all those jocks and cheerleaders, and Shay, of course."

"Shay." I shake my head. "You know my dad left?"

"No. Sorry, Tyler."

"All because Shay convinced Mom to be a feminist, and got her the cafeteria job, and made us laughingstocks." I turn toward Evie. "Do you know the last time my mom made dinner? You wouldn't know that either, would you? You're never over anymore."

"You never invite me over."

"Come over next Saturday night. We're throwing a kegger for Shay's birthday."

"A kegger? How did you get your parents to agree to that?"

"They won't find out. My dad's in an apartment in Sherman Oaks. He won't come back unless my mom quits her job, which she refuses to do. My mom is going to this crazy Wimyn's Fulfillment Retreat Shay got her to sign up for. Our party's going to be, like, a blowout. Besides being Shay's birthday party, this is my, like, coming out party with the popular people."

"Do you realize you just used the word 'like' twice? You're actually talking just like Shay now," Evie says.

I cross my arms. "You think being cool is bad."

"Yes," Evie says. "If 'cool' means ditching your friends." She crosses her arms too.

The bus stops short at a light, jolting us back and forth, but neither of us uncrosses our arms. We ride with our arms crossed all the way to school. Then I get off the bus without another word to Evie.

Debbie M. meets me at the sidewalk. "Ty Ty!" She puts her arms around me and squeezes. Oh, that sour smell. Does she rub lemons all over herself? Bathe in lemon juice? "I missed you sooo much since yesterday," she coos.

I watch Shay walk onto campus. It looks like she taped up the thrift store dress at least half a foot.

"Did you miss me, Ty Ty?"

Where does Shay go all day besides physics class and the lunch area?

"Ty Ty, tell me you missed me."

Evie is staggering past the school office under her loaded backpack. I wonder if Evie and I will ever talk again.

"Earth calling Ty Ty." Debbie M. pats my cheek.

It stings from Shay's slap. I try not to wince.

"Are you there, Ty Ty?"

"I'm there. Here. Like, whatever." Gawd, I really am talking like Shay. "Sorry. I, uh . . ." I free myself from Debbie M.'s grip. "I have to go to class."

24

The doorbell rings. I'm bent over the kitchen counter, arranging the celery and carrots around my homemade blue cheese dip in a pinwheel pattern like I saw Mrs. Gray do before she gave up that sort of thing. My party doesn't start for fifteen more minutes and I'm still in the gingham apron Mrs. Gray made for me. But I get the door anyway.

It's Rick, bearing gifts. "Hey, sweetie."

Sweetie. Nice. "You're early, actually." *Actually? Actually, I'm talking like Tyler.*

"I thought you might want a hand getting ready," Rick says. "Hey, I like tonight's apron better than the one for Krasno's Diner."

"Can you untie it?"

"Sure." He sets down the gifts and comes around behind me. "Not only are you good in the kitchen, but, man, you have a great ass."

"Thanks." I'm wearing my fashionably, murderously tight Calvin Kleins, which I had to lie on my bed and inhale just to zip up.

"Happy eighteenth birthday." Rick hands me one of the presents, sloppily wrapped in smiley face paper. Inside is a Led Zeppelin cassette tape. "It's got 'Stairway to Heaven' on it," he says. I thank him and hope the next gift's better.

It is. It's a dainty gold bracelet with great charms on it: a chef's hat, probably because I work in a diner and they don't make sponge charms; a heart; the number *18*; the letter *S*; and a book.

I go to kiss him, but he hands me the last present, a bottle of champagne. He puts his arms around me. "Later do you want to get in the bath with me again?"

"Hi, Shay. Hey, Rick," Tyler says like it's no big deal that I'm being propositioned in his house. He looks good tonight in the surfer shirt and 501s I picked out for him at the mall.

"The Tyster," Rick says.

"Can you set up the keg?" Tyler points to the backyard and Rick heads outside.

"You look great," I tell Tyler.

"Thanks." His voice is flat. "I rigged up a fan to go at an extreme velocity and in reverse." He stares at a spot on the wall to my right. "It would just take me a few minutes to duct-tape it to the bathroom ceiling. I can do it anytime. If you don't want to leave The Di—Rick, bring him in the bathtub with you."

"But—"

"Whatever will get you home."

"I feel like I am home."

"Well, you're not."

Heather comes into the kitchen wearing the outfit I helped her choose, a new red minidress, a white cardigan purposefully shrunk in the dryer, and hot red high heel shoes.

"You look bitchin'," I tell her.

"Thanks. So do you."

Mariel arrives next. She looks bitchin' too. She's in the clothes we bought last week—a black skirt from the thrift shop, which she's hemmed four inches, and a shimmering violet blouse from Mervyn's. I did an awesome job on her makeup this afternoon.

"Happy birthday." She hands me a gift. "Is book Spanish poems."

"Awesome." I actually mean it. "Thanks. Come on in. Have some crudités. That means carrots and celery. I just learned that word myself a few weeks ago."

We walk to the kitchen. "You are no happy," Mariel says.

"Tyler wants me to leave." I return my apron to its drawer.

"For real?" She pats my back, which is a reach for her, being such a shrimp.

"He doesn't see me reading and studying physics and working with you at Krasno's. He doesn't know how much I've changed."

"You tell him," she says.

I shake my head. "Do you know what Einstein said? That mystery is the most beautiful thing. I found that in one of Tyler's books. He's a big Einstein nut. But I don't think Tyler finds the mystery surrounding me beautiful at all."

"¿Qué?"

I sigh. "He has the right to be pissed off. He thinks I destroyed his parents' marriage. I was just trying to help."

"You help me. You help me much."

"Just keep going to school, okay?"

"Okay. School is okay." She smiles. "Is your birthday. Try be happy."

I nod, take a deep breath, which is difficult in my tight Calvins, and yell, "Let's get this party started!"

"Music?" Heather calls back. "What album should I play?"

"It's my birthday, so please don't play Neil Diamond, Barry Manilow, or anything disco."

She puts on "Stairway to Heaven."

A half hour later, kids are crowding into the house. It seems like half the school is here—the popular crowd, Heather's student government friends, a lot of guys now crushing on her, and Tyler's old honor club friends, who huddle around my vegetable platter.

I lose track of Rick and Mariel and Heather, so I wander outside. The backyard is hopping with my school lunch group: Lori, Debby with a y, and Debbie P., all in tight designer jeans like me; one of the Lisas, making out on the glider with an older, bearded guy; Jeff in brown corduroy pants, smoking a cigarette; and Jim and John, sharing a joint. Heather's by the lamppost, surrounded by three boys about her age. She's holding an empty plastic cup and she's wobbly either from her high heels or the beer or both.

One of the boys switches out Heather's empty cup for one filled with beer. "Try again. See if you can down it in ten seconds."

"Ten. Nine. Eight," the boys chant.

"Wait!" I shout.

Heather stops drinking and the boys stop counting.

"Don't do that to yourself," I tell her.

"Everything's more fun when you drink. You said that."

"Go for it," one of the guys calls out.

Heather pours more beer down her throat.

"Seven. Six. Five."

"Heather, no!" I grab the half-full cup from her and make the boys leave. "You're too young to chug beer like that," I tell her. "Actually, you shouldn't drink at all." *Actually*.

"You should talk," she says.

"There you are, Shay." John slinks in between us. "And Heather, man, you look foxy tonight." He puts his arm around her, stares at her cleavage. "I dig that sweater. It shows off your . . . your . . . uh, eyes. You're really, uh, growing up."

She laughs. Her laugh has changed. It's the giggle of a girl acting dumb. Holy crap, she's flirting with John!

I shake my head. "You two can barely hold yourselves up. And, John, do you realize Heather's only fifteen?"

"Almost sixteen," Heather says.

"Let's go find a couch," John takes Heather's hand. "Put our feet up and get cozy."

"No. Leave my sister alone." Tyler gets between them.

"Dude, mellow out."

"I can take care of myself," Heather says.

Tyler gets in John's face. "Don't make me mad."

"Okay, okay." He flashes a peace sign. "Make love not war, man."

Tyler glares at me. "I hope you're proud of yourself now."

Debbie M. throws her arms around his waist from behind. "Ty Ty, I've been looking for you. Deb Deb's wonewee."

"What?" He doesn't seem exactly thrilled, but he doesn't move away either.

"She's wonewee." I roll my eyes. "That's baby talk for *lonely*."

"I think you've had too much beer," he says, but doesn't stop her from groping him.

What have I done?

What have I done?

Debbie M. is leaning against my back, attempting to undo my Levi's. Thank God I'm wearing button-up 501s and she's had too much to drink.

Wait a minute. What am I thinking? I'm upset because a pretty girl is trying to get into my pants? I've been dreaming of something like this happening ever since my voice started changing. And while Debbie M. plays with my pants, I'm throwing a cool party with the most popular kids in school. This is what I longed for all those Saturday nights when Evie and I played backgammon or watched *Star Wars* with our other dweeb friends.

I wonder if Evie ever saw *Star Wars* that night she

called. Who would she have gone with? Maybe some of the guys she's been sitting with at lunch. I wonder what Evie's doing tonight.

My chest aches again. It's probably heartburn from that awful beer I swallowed before spitting into the grass. Shay said I just needed to get used to the taste, but there's no way I'm trying it again.

Oh, crud, Debbie M.'s actually got my pants button undone. *You mean "Oh, good,"* I lecture myself.

She whispers, "Does Ty Ty have a bedroom we could use?"

Ty Ty? Bedroom? No! Not with Debbie M.

Tyler, I remind myself, *this is what you wanted.*

I guess I changed my mind. I turn around and put my hands over Debbie M.'s. "Stop."

"Debbie M. is pretty, popular, and pickled," a voice behind me says. "You should be ecstatic, Tyler."

I turn around again and see Evie. My chest thumps. I didn't think she would actually come to the party. She looks different tonight. It's hard to tell by the muted light of the lamppost, but something's strange about her face. "What are you doing here?" I ask. "You look kind of weird."

"Who's she?" Debbie M. says from behind me.

"I'm nobody, really. At least in your little world," Evie says. "Tyler invited me. If it's a problem, I'll leave right now."

"It's a problem," Debbie M. says.

"Mind your own business, Deb Deb." I button up my Levi's and step toward Evie. "You're totally welcome here, Evie. Don't you know that?"

"You have a strange way of showing it." For some reason, her lips are orange and puffy. Are they sneering or trembling? "You asked me what I'm doing here. You told me I . . ." The bottom one is definitely trembling, like an earthquake.

"Evie, what the heck is wrong with you tonight?"

"You told me I look weird."

"No. I said '*kind of* weird.' I'm sorry. I didn't mean it that way." My chest is killing me. I may be highly allergic to beer.

"She does look weird," Debbie M. says. "It's like she put on five coats of makeup in the dark."

"Makeup? My God, Evie! You're wearing makeup."

"Badly," Debbie M. says.

"You . . ." Evie sniffs. "You didn't . . ." She sounds like she's choking.

"What's gotten into you?" I ask her.

"You didn't even appreciate it." Then she does something even weirder than wearing makeup. She starts crying, just like a girl. Black mascara and brown and green eye shadow, or whatever is in the vicinity of her eyes, run down her face. She wipes the mess with her hand, which mixes the eye stuff with the red gunk on her cheeks.

I stand in front of her, clutching my chest, which feels

like it's about to explode. I hate when girls cry. I hate even more that Evie's crying.

"Are you okay?" Shay's voice comes from behind Debbie M., who's still behind me.

Evie nods, but she's still crying.

"Gawd, Tyler, at least give her a hug," Shay says.

I take a clumsy step forward with my arms out.

Evie takes a step back. "Where's that twenty dollars you owe me?"

"I would have repaid you," I tell her. "But Shay stole my money."

"I have to barf," Debbie M. says.

I point to the trash can and say, "Bye." She lurches away.

Shay reaches into the pocket of her jeans. Her pants are so tight she has to wriggle her hand in and suck in her little stomach to get anything out. She comes up with a twenty-dollar bill. "I wish I could give you the rest now. Here's a start."

She hands me the money and I give it to Evie. "Just don't ask Shay where she got it. She'll slap you."

"You can be such an ass, Tyler," Shay says.

Someone claps my back, hard, so I turn around. It's The Dick. "Tyster. Are you upsetting my girlfriend?"

I shake my head because it's hard to talk while a huge guy with his hand on your back is accusing you of upsetting his girlfriend. Not to mention after you just saw your best friend in heavy makeup and heavier tears, suddenly realized your best friend has girl qualities, were just called an ass, and are suffering possible heart attack symptoms at age eighteen.

"We need to talk. Come out to my car with me," The Dick says.

Yikes. For issues of personal safety, I'd rather remain at the party, within shouting range of potential witnesses. "I wish I could sit in your souped-up Mustang," I lie. "But—"

"Let's boogie." He pushes me forward.

Don't they usually take people for a ride just before killing them, like in the *Godfather* movies? On the other hand, I'm more terrified to turn him down. I think The Dick just made me an offer I can't refuse. "Okay, I'll come out to your car with you," I say loudly, hoping plenty of witnesses will hear me and testify in the assault trial later.

"Here, Shay." Evie holds out the twenty-dollar bill. "I didn't mean to pressure you about the money. If you need it, I can wait."

I keep my hands at my sides. "Hang on to it. I really appreciate you convincing Mrs. Gray to take me in. I want to pay Tyler back the rest of his money too."

"Well, thanks." She frowns. "I bet my stupid crying jag messed up my makeup. Tonight's the first time I've worn it."

No kidding. "Let's go wash your face."

There's a huge line for the downstairs bathroom, so we head upstairs and stand behind five other people. "What made you put makeup on?" I ask Evie.

"Oh." She looks away. "A scientific experiment?"

"It was for Tyler, right?"

"What?" If her cheeks hadn't had a ton of rouge on them already, I think I would have seen her blushing.

"I'm not a genius," I tell Evie. "But I'm pretty sure you're in love with your best friend."

She frowns. "Former best friend. Could you give me that makeover you were talking about before?"

"You don't need it."

"But Tyler—"

"Listen, Evie. You don't want a guy who just cares about your looks. You want a guy who loves you for who you are. Like, a guy who doesn't even mind if you wear an apron and carry books around and put your hair up in a pony to scrub pots and pans."

"But Tyler—"

"Tyler may have a big brain, but he needs to think with it for a change."

"Get in," The Dick says as we approach his Mustang.

I get in. I'm so scared, my brain's gone numb. I warn my leg not to shake, but my leg doesn't listen. I leave the car door open.

Rick reaches over me with his bulky and quite hairy arms, possibly to grab my neck and shake me like a squawking chicken.

Instead, he slams the car door shut. His huge body practically takes up the whole driver's side. He has a great build. I can almost see why Shay digs him. Not that I'm into checking out other males, but it helps keep my mind off thoughts of getting hit.

"Are you sleeping with my girlfriend?" he asks.

My leg is shaking like Jiffy Pop. "No, Di—Rick. Never."

"Never?" It comes out like a growl.

"I mean, not that she isn't desirable."

He bares his teeth at me.

"She's been sleeping in Heather's room. Shay and I, we're actually more like sister and brother."

"You're not lying to me, are you? Because Debbie M. said—"

"Debbie M.'s drunk, and she's mad I wouldn't let her pull down my pants, and . . . Rick, Shay likes *you*, not me."

"Really? Did she tell you she likes me? I mean, really likes me?" He doesn't sound so tough now. I never knew anyone from the popular table could sound like this. Especially The Dick. He's supposed to be cocky, not gawky.

"Tell me she loves me."

I've told enough lies the last few weeks. I take a deep breath. "I don't think she loves any guys. I think she sort of uses guys, to tell you the truth." I hope he doesn't believe in shooting the messenger, or even beating up the messenger, the messenger being me. I take a deep breath. "Sorry, D—Rick."

He pounds the steering wheel. "It's because I'm so stupid. I just couldn't understand all that weird science stuff."

"Physics?"

"I don't know. Maybe. She's always going on about magnet fields, and waves or something, and stuff she reads."

"What? Shay? Seriously?"

"I didn't understand half the things she said."

If I weren't within striking distance of The Dick right now, I'd be smiling.

"She's too good for me," he moans.

Before I realize the extreme risk I'm taking, I put my hand on his arm. It feels like it's made of metal.

"What are you doing?" he says.

What *am* I doing? I shouldn't touch a huge guy with steel arms. I drop my hand down and sit on it. "Sorry."

"No. I'm sorry. I wish I was as smart as Shay." He's shaking his head right and left.

Maybe he's not actually a dick. Maybe Shay had slightly better taste than I gave her credit for. Maybe I should help the poor guy before he bursts into tears. It could happen. After watching Evie cry tonight, I'd believe just about anything. "I think, actually, she likes you a lot. Just, like, give her some time."

"Really?" His head slows down.

"Yeah."

"Thanks, Tyster."

"Anytime, bud."

"You can get out of my car now." He leans over me again and opens the door.

I scramble out and return to the party.

I search for Evie, but it's hard amid the noise and crowds. "Stairway to Heaven" is playing again, and a group in the living room is chanting "Chug it." The nasty smell of beer permeates everything. In the kitchen, someone's spilled the blue cheese dip all over the counter, which doesn't improve on the beer smell.

I look for Evie in the backyard. I know my odds of actually finding her there are low, given that (1) it's packed with people, (2) she's little, and (3) it's dark. I wish everyone but Evie would leave right now.

Wait a minute. Aren't I supposed to be enjoying this?

Yeah, well, I'm not. As Shay would say, *Whatever.*

I go inside and upstairs and into my bedroom, shoo out two juniors with their shirts off and their hands down each other's jeans, and close my door.

I try to read *The Great Gatsby* for English class, but it's hard to root for a guy who's screwing up his life just to impress people.

Someone knocks on my door.

"Off limits!"

"It's me. Shay."

I open the door.

"You said you could get me back to 2006. I'm ready to go now."

Good, I guess.

"There's a line for the bathroom," she says. "You can do this fast, right?"

I nod. "Are you sure you want to do this?" I can't help asking her.

"You think I messed up everything for you here. Your dad left, you and Evie aren't friends anymore, Heather's drinking. I'm really sorry." She walks into my room and closes the door behind her. "You want me out of here, right?"

I stare at my poster of Albert Einstein. He was a man who got things done. "Yes, I still want you to leave."

"Okay." She looks like I've just slapped her, which is ironic because she recently slapped me.

"So you'll follow my directions and return home." I don't ask it. I order it. Like Dad used to do before he moved out. I get the box from my closet containing the fan, scissors, and duct tape.

We walk down the hall in silence and stand in line for the bathroom. "Mariel!" Shay exclaims to a short Mexican girl who lines up behind us. "You okay? I lost track of you."

"I am good." She looks at me. "Is Tyler?"

"Yes," Shay says. "Tyler, this is Mariel. Mariel, Tyler."

"Do you go to our school?" I ask her.

"I start school yesterday. Shay, she talk me in it."

Huh? Why would Shay do that? She doesn't even go to school herself, except for physics class. "How did you meet her?" I ask Mariel.

"We work Krasno's Diner. We clear tables and wash dishes. She teach me the English too."

I bet the circumference of my open mouth right now is at least five inches.

"She need money to pay back you."

Holy moly. So that's where she got her money. Shay Saunders did menial labor.

"She say owe you," Mariel says.

And I owe her. An apology.

I'm about to tell Shay I'm sorry when Heather stumbles out of the bathroom like a Gumby doll and the girl in front of us goes in. Heather clutches my arm. "I don't feel too good." Her breath is sour from smoke and beer.

I glare at Shay. "You see why you have to go?"

"Go where?" Heather asks.

"Far away. She messed up our whole family."

"Mom's a lot happier," Heather says.

"Say what?"

"Didn't you hear her crying all the time before? She was miserable. Shay made Mom brave enough to do what she really wanted. Don't go, Shay," Heather pleads.

"It was Tyler who actually invited me here in the first place. I've already worn out my welcome mat or whatever with him," Shay says.

"Shay messed up my life," I tell Heather.

"Poor you. Looking a lot better, eating lunch with the cool people, dating Debbie M."

"Ugh. We're not really dating. And Evie's barely talking to me."

"Because you blew her off. That's your fault."

The bathroom door opens and the girl walks out. I pick up the box and step forward. "Let's go. Let's do it."

I hope I'm not making a mistake.

He's making a mistake.

Tyler turns on the bathwater, then stands on the ledge of the tub, duct-taping the fan to the ceiling. "Once you leave, everything should revert to how it was."

"I think you're wrong," I say.

"It's the best I could do. It's battery-operated, and I rigged it to go extremely fast."

"I think I changed people for good."

"For bad." He frowns. "Would you mind removing your clothes? I'll try not to look."

"You've seen me naked before. What's the big deal?" But it is a big deal. I don't take my clothes off so easily anymore.

I remove everything but my undergarments. He steps off the bathtub ledge and sets the scissors and what's left of the roll of duct tape on the bathroom floor.

Someone knocks. "Use the bathroom downstairs," Tyler yells.

"The fan isn't going to send me back in time, anyway," I say. "The tides don't work like that."

He looks at me, blushes when he sees me half naked, and turns away. "We didn't learn about tides in physics class."

"I've been reading books, Tyler. What did you think I was doing every morning at school? You said I wasn't stupid."

"You're not." He looks at me again, this time holding his gaze on my eyes.

I stare right back at him. "Albert Einstein himself said time travel would have to reach the speed of light. There's no way you can rig a fan to go that fast."

"Then how did you get here in the first place?" he asks.

"I don't think physics or science had anything to do with it. The force was a lot bigger than physics. As Einstein said, 'The intellect should not be made—' "

" 'Our god,' " I say. " 'The intellect should not be made our god.' You read one of my books about Einstein."

"Two of them." She smiles. "Actually."

I have to grab the wall to steady myself.

But if Shay's correct and a super-charged fan didn't send her through time, then how the heck did she get here? Einstein also said the most incomprehensible thing about the world is that it is at all comprehensible. Maybe we'll never know why Shay came here. Maybe it was meant to be. Einstein was passionate about science, but he also believed in God.

"I'll get in the bathtub if you want to try out your plan. If you still want me gone." She removes her bra and panties and climbs into the warm tub.

"I don't *want* you gone, actually, but you *have* to go. Don't you?"

"Let me be honest, for once in my life. Besides wanting to help people here, there's also a selfish reason I'd like to stay." She takes a big breath. "I deserve your family. I deserve a sister like Heather, and a mother like Mrs. Gray, and you, Tyler. And, believe it or not, Rick's a good guy and I deserve him too. I know I acted like a jerk before, ditching school and sleeping around and yelling at Mariel and all that crap. I guess I thought I didn't deserve a better life, a classy one. Then Mrs. Gray said I was sweet, and you asked me for help with physics and *The Great Gatsby*, like I really could help you, and Heather actually looked up to me. Actually. And Rick treated me like I was worth something too."

"Of course you're worth something. You're worth a lot."

"I deserve your family. I deserve Rick. I deserve you. And, Tyler, if you ever stopped sulking and blaming and being so stupid, you might just deserve me too."

Someone knocks again. "Shay, could you put your clothes back on?" I never thought I'd be telling a beautiful girl to put her clothes back on. "I'm going to get rid of this stupid fan. You're right. It won't work. And, like, I wouldn't want it to work anyway."

She gets dressed in a hurry and we walk out with the fan. There's a huge line for the bathroom. "Sorry about holding you up," I say before a guy rushes in.

I point to the fan inside the box and tell Shay, "I'm going to put this outside in the trash can. You should go find Rick. He loves you, Shay."

She kisses me on the cheek. "And what are you going to do after you throw out the fan?" she asks.

"Probably resume reading *The Great Gatsby*."

"Oh, I can tell you about it. Gatsby was an idiot. He gave himself a makeover when he should have just, like, stayed who he was. It's hard to explain. The dude dies in the end."

"Thanks a lot."

"You're not actually going to hide out in your room during your own party, are you?"

"Well, yeah. Shay, I thought I'd really like partying with the popular people. But actually, I'd rather be doing what I used to do on Saturday nights, playing backgammon with Evie. Or going to the movies with Evie. Or, actually, doing anything with Evie. Sometimes we just hung out. That was fun too."

"Where is she?"

I shrug. "She's so little. There's no way I can find her in this crowd."

"Aren't you even going to try?"

"I . . . She's mad at me. And she's acting strange. She put all this makeup on her face."

"Why do you think she did that, Tyler?"

I shake my head. "It doesn't make sense."

"Gawd, Tyler, for a smart guy you're really dumb. Okay, what color eyes does she have?"

"What? I don't know. She wears glasses."

"Behind those glasses she has two things called eyes, Tyler."

I sigh. "I never thought to really look before."

She shakes her head. "Exactly. Now go toss that fan, find Evie, apologize, and figure out why she's wearing makeup and what color eyes she actually has."

"Actually?"

She grins. "Yeah, bro. Actually. I'm going to look for Rick."

After she leaves, I search all through the backyard and inside the house. But Evie's gone.

I get out of bed at eight A.M. because my blue cheese dip/beer/overnight breath smells gnarly, Heather's snoring loudly, I'm craving Tab badly, and I need to clean the house.

After wrapping myself in Mrs. Gray's old robe, I head to the bathroom. It's a wreck. The counter is littered with plastic cups, some still full of beer. The sink contains cigarette butts and black hairs. The mirror is so grungy, I can barely see myself in it. I brush my teeth, but skip my hair and shower because there's a ton of work to do.

The downstairs reeks, mostly of beer, but also of tobacco and clove cigarettes and pot. Luckily, Mrs. Gray isn't due home for nine more hours. I grab a Tab and gulp it down as I go from room to room opening windows. Then I pick up trash: a million plastic cups, napkins, directions to our house, half-eaten celery sticks, and a condom still in its wrapper, which I pocket, making a mental note: *Do not leave condom in Mrs. Gray's robe!*

After that, I wipe the kitchen counters and table, sticky from beer and dip and God knows what else. Then I get out the Pledge and polish the wood furniture just like Mrs. Gray showed me. I'm making everything shine.

174

* * *

At first I think that I'm not really downstairs, that I'm in my bed having a crazy dream. Because Shay is not only polishing the furniture and humming "Stairway to Heaven," she's actually smiling while she does it. But, no, it's really her, with oily hair and an ugly robe, and it appears she's already picked up the trash. "Wow. Thanks for getting an early jump on this mess," I tell her.

"I'm working at the diner from noon to three today—Rick's driving me—so I'm helping out here now. How about you start on the bathrooms?"

"You mean cleaning them?"

"No. Teaching them to dance."

"Cleaning is supposed to be woman's work," I tell Shay. "My mom and Heather always do it."

"If you want girls to like you, you'd better stop acting like the damn king of the house."

"I guess you're right." I sigh. "Look where it got my father."

"Exactly."

We bring the cleaning supplies into the downstairs bathroom. Shay tells me which stuff to use where, lectures me about germs, and gives me demos.

"I thought your old housekeeper did all the cleaning," I say.

"Your mom's been teaching me this stuff. She's pretty cool."

I elbow her. "Isn't calling a parent *cool* a violation of one of your social rules?"

"It's the exception that probes the rule. Or however that goes. Whatever." She hands me the toilet bowl cleaner and a long plastic brush. "You can start here."

I squirt blue stuff into the toilet. "Are you just going to stand over me, watching?"

"Yep." She puts her hand through her ratty hair. "I'm entitled to a break. Make sure you scrub hard."

"You know what I'd appreciate more than cleaning tips?" I ask.

"Advice on girls?"

"Yeah, that too. But how about some stock tips?"

"That's totally beyond me. As if I even understand— Wait. I already told you about Starbucks and Microsoft. Wal-Mart's good too. But stay away from the airlines. They're always in bankruptcy. We can go through the business section of the newspaper later."

"Thanks."

"But I'd like a favor from you in return," she says. "Can you make me some fake documents so I can enroll in school? If you can't do it on your computer, your genius friend Evie might be able to figure something out. As long as I'm going to be here awhile, I might as well learn stuff."

"Sure, Shay. What the heck is that?" It sounds like the

garage door is opening, but that's impossible. "Mom's not supposed to be here until dinnertime."

"Holy crap. We still have to finish the bathrooms and vacuum the house and do the upstairs and the backyard." Shay grabs the 409, sprays the bathroom counter, and wipes it furiously.

I flush the toilet to get rid of the blue stuff and dart out of the room toward the backyard.

"Tyler."

Oh my God, it's Dad. He's walking into the living room dragging a suitcase, the biggest one we own, as if he'd planned on being gone a long time. He looks thin and he's got gray, puffy semicircles under his eyes. "Where's your mother?" he asks.

"She should be home early evening."

"Where is she?"

I hunch my shoulders. "At this Wimyn's Fulfillment Retreat in Ojai."

"She's at what?" He sighs. "I guess I wasn't exactly fulfilling her."

I stare at the suitcase at Dad's feet. "Are you back, Dad? I mean, for good?"

"If your mother will have me," he says.

"She hasn't quit the cafeteria job." I picture Mom in her hairnet, smiling as she doles out mashed potatoes and urges the kids not to fill up on starch.

"Are people still asking you if we need money?"

"A few. But actually, Dad, who cares? We could try

to impress people, or we could just do what makes us happy."

"Your mother makes me happy," he says. "And so do you and your sister."

Shay comes out of the bathroom. "Your family makes me happy too."

"You're still here." This doesn't seem to make Dad happy. "What's that?" He points to the bulging trash bags in the kitchen. Then he looks down. Even the shag carpeting doesn't hide the potato chip crumbs and dirt carried in from the backyard. "You had a party here last night, didn't you?"

I can't think of a good lie. I look to Shay for help.

"Yes, we had my birthday party here last night," she says. "It's my fault. I'm sorry."

"Me too," I say.

Dad looks all around the family room and kitchen. "Did anything get broken or stolen?"

"Not that I know of," I tell him.

"I hope for your sakes nothing did," he says. "I want your mother in a good mood today when she sees me. I'll help you take out the trash. Then you'd better clean this mess. And don't ever do this again."

"I don't mean to interfere." Shay says.

"Since when did you not mean to interfere?" I ask her.

She punches me lightly on the arm. "Anyway, Mr. Gray, you should buy your wife a nice bouquet. Women love flowers. But not cheap ones like carnations or daisies. Roses, maybe, or you can try something more exotic. And have you ever thought about thinning out your moustache? Also, you should stop reading the newspaper at the dinner table."

Dad looks at me. "How long is she staying here?" he asks.

"A long time." I smile.

26

"Come on, already," Shay says. "I've got to help your dad make dinner before Mom gets home."

"Can't we practice one more time?"

"For God's sake, we've gone over this to death. What's the number?" She grabs the phone. "I'll dial. Even though I hate stupid dials."

I take the receiver from Shay. "You sure I should do this?"

She rolls her eyes. "Yes. Gawd. Hurry up. You want privacy?"

"No, I want coaching. Stay right here." I dial the number.

"Hello?"

"Hey, Evie. I was looking for you last night."

There's a pause. "Why?" she says.

"Why?" I glare at Shay. We didn't prepare for Evie asking why. "Uh, well, because I wanted to hang out with you."

"What about all your new, popular friends?"

I didn't think Evie would ask me this question either. "I like some of them too. Not all of them, but . . . Listen, Evie, I want to return to our old lunch table."

"Why?"

Good Lord, will the girl ever stop interrogating me? "I

like joking around with you, playing backgammon, talking physics, not having to worry if I'm wearing the right shoes. And I really . . ." I look at Shay. She nods, so I continue. "I really miss you, Evie."

"I miss you too."

There goes that heartburn again. I guess it wasn't the beer. "Evie, you want to see *Star Wars* with me Saturday night?"

Shay shoves my shoulder.

I clear my throat. "We could have dinner first."

"We haven't been to Sambos in a long time," Evie says.

"I was thinking of somewhere nicer. There's this French restaurant in Encino. Jean-Paul's?"

"That fancy place?"

"Yeah, we could dress up. It could be like a date."

She doesn't say anything.

"Evie?"

"You want me to get all dressed up?"

"You don't have to. We could go somewhere else." Shay shoves me again. "On our date," I add.

"I don't actually own anything really nice. You think your friend Shay could take me shopping?"

"Next time I see Shay I could ask." I smirk. Shay smirks back. "So is this Saturday night okay? Dinner and a late movie? I have to find out from my parents whether I have a curfew."

"Really?"

"It's probably fine with them. I'm even hoping I can borrow my dad's sports car."

"No. I meant *Really, this is a date?*" she asks.

"Well, actually, like, yeah, it's a date. I mean, if you want it to be."

"Okay."

Okay. Was there ever a better word uttered? "And, Evie," I add. "Maybe Shay could help you find an outfit to bring out your pretty hazel eyes."

"Shay," he says after hanging up the phone. "Did I ever thank you for changing my life?"

"No. Mostly you complained about it."

"Then today let me formally express my gratitude. Thank you, Shay. Really." He says it like he means it.

"Right back at you," I tell him. Then we hug, leaving half a foot between us. "I guess God or whoever knew what She was doing when She sent me here."

"She?" He raises his eyebrows. They could use a little re-trimming.

"If it even was God who actually sent me here," I say.

He shrugs. "I have, like, no idea."

"I think I'm here for a reason. God does not play dice. Albert Einstein said that."

He nods. "And Einstein also said that a person exists for other people. So do me a big favor, Shay. Just to be safe, from now on take showers, not baths."

"Good idea." I smile at him and he smiles back.